ROYAL
SECRET

ROYAL SECRET

The Secret Royals
Book 2

MARIE LONG

ROYAL
SECRET

CHAPTER I

I'M HERE. I CAN'T BELIEVE IT.

I was just a small-town South Carolina girl who always had big dreams. But who knew dreams could ever become real? Mine had come to life in the form of an online ten-day vacation giveaway and a handsome six-foot-four hunk named Erudito, who wore a classy chauffeur's outfit. *"Trina Mauer Vacations in Style"—sounds like the next big-hit television series.* I grinned at the thought.

From under the brim of his black chauffeur's hat, Erudito stared at me in the rearview mirror with enticing brown eyes. As soon as our eyes met, his gaze returned to the road.

I inhaled the rich scent of leather as I ran my hand across the soft upholstery of the limousine's backseat. Last year, I'd told my best friend, Claudia Gray, that we would see each other again soon. *Who knew it'd be* this *soon?* Needless to say, Claudia was just as ecstatic as I was when I told her that I'd won the two-week getaway to Bellacigna sponsored by my favorite romance author, international bestseller M.E. Stacson.

The ride from the airport offered a magnificent view of Bellacigna's picturesque countryside. Claudia had described it as something straight out of a storybook. She wasn't kidding. The trees, full and vibrantly green, stood among endless fields of colorful wildflowers, small farms, and rustic, Italian-style vineyards. My hotel was located in Fiore Luna, a city located thirty miles from the airport and about fifteen minutes from the city of Cittàcigni, where Claudia and her husband, Stefano, lived. Luck would have it that she'd gotten hitched to a handsome Bellacignan like Stefano Trevisani—who also happened to be a *royal duke* in disguise. I wished my life was half as exciting as hers. But not much excitement happened to a barista at a small-town mom-and-pop coffee shop from eight to five.

As we rode into Fiore Luna's outskirts, the top of a giant skyscraper came into view, stretching high above all the others, making it one of the tallest points in the city. The building's windows glittered, reflecting the sun like hundreds of little stars on a pillar. I would've never pegged it for a hotel if I hadn't noticed the impressive gold-plated sign out front that read Verde Suites.

"Whoa! *This* is where I'm staying?" My voice squeaked.

Erudito's eyes met mine again in the rearview mirror. "*Sì, signorina.* Verde Suites is Fiore Luna's premier five-star hotel."

I blinked several times. *I must be dreaming.* I pinched myself just to make sure… nope. The situation was definitely as real as things got. I took a deep breath to calm my nerves. "So what do you recommend I see or do while I'm here, Erudito?"

His brown eyes flicked to mine, the corners wrinkling slightly as he smiled. "*Gelaterie* are a popular thing in this country. Fiore Luna has a really good one about five blocks from your hotel. You should really try the *Di Martina Migliori*. It is a rich chocolate flavor. Very popular."

I raised an eyebrow. "Really? A chocolate gelato is all the rage around here? I won't believe it till I see it—er, taste it."

"Would you like me to drive you there now, signorina?"

While chocolate gelato sounded tempting, it was best that I checked in at the hotel and got settled first. Perhaps I would try to make it to a *gelaterie* sometime the next day, during one of the few breaks in my almost-full schedule. I'd blocked out a lot of time in my planner for sightseeing and activities. Two weeks definitely wasn't long enough to see and do everything. "No, I really should check in to the hotel instead."

"Of course."

I glanced out the window at the strip of quaint shops and cafés that we passed. "How's the nightlife here?"

"Quite lively, signorina. The most popular hotspots are the local jazz lounges."

That certainly piqued my interest. "Really? I love jazz. Any places close by?"

"Sì. There is one just a block from the hotel called Heaven and Blues. Feel free to call me if you would like me to drive you there."

I fingered the business card in my purse, the one Erudito had given me when he'd picked me up at the airport. I would feel awkward calling a chauffeur to drive me one block. Though I had no intentions of bothering him like that, I kept the thought in mind that he would be at my beck and call for the duration of my stay.

Erudito pulled up to the hotel entrance, and two attendants rushed to the car. One carried a sign with the letter *T* written in fancy calligraphy and set it in front of the car. Erudito jumped out and hustled around to open the door for me. I took his offered hand and got out of the car with exaggerated grace, like the red carpet celebrities do—because I had *always* wanted to do that. The attendants loaded my two large suitcases and garment bag onto a fancy gold luggage cart and quickly wheeled it inside the hotel.

"Signorina." Erudito's voice was so close to my ear that I started. He gestured toward the main entrance, and after one glance back at the parked limo, I headed for the doors.

"Why did the hotel staff put a sign in front of the car like that?" I asked, feeling totally clueless.

He walked just a few steps behind me. "It is used by the Trevisani family to denote that the space is reserved."

I halted before the entrance. *Trevisani.* "Did you say Trevisani? As in the Trevisani Royals of Bellacigna?"

"Sì. Though you are not of the royal family, I was instructed to ensure that the sign was placed out."

More questions swarmed through my head, but before I could ask anything else, Erudito gestured for me to continue inside. I was only a few steps away from the revolving glass door when my foot caught on the doorstep. My body pitched forward toward the door, and my heart dropped in my gut as I struggled to keep my balance. I yelped, but the anticipated painful impact never came. Instead, a strong arm grabbed me and pulled me away from the revolving door just as one of them whooshed inches past my face. The smell of leather with undertones of cedarwood touched my senses. I felt Erudito's warmth and rigid body as he steadied me. I put my hand over his for support and stared down at the beautiful contrast of my sandy-brown skin complementing his olive complexion. My cheeks burned. *Great. Erudito must think I'm the biggest klutz now.*

"Are you okay?" he asked in a soft, concerned voice.

I swallowed and nodded, unable to speak.

"Do be careful, signorina," he said, gently steadying me on my feet.

"Thank you," I managed to whisper.

He released me. "I will inform the management of that hazardous step." He led the way inside this time, scanning the area for any more hazards, and I followed.

Stepping through the revolving doors was like stepping through a portal to a magical castle.

Glittering chandeliers sent tiny dots of rainbow-colored light dancing about the floor and cream-colored walls of the massive lobby. The blue-marble floors shone like glass despite the constant traffic of hotel guests and workers.

The lobby opened up into a massive atrium that extended above and beyond what my eyes could see. Glass elevators on both ends of the atrium provided access to the many floors above. My mouth hung open as I ogled. If I wasn't careful, I would drool on this expensive-looking floor.

After I checked in, a well-dressed bellhop approached me. He was young, charming, and smiling as though he really loved his job. "*Buonasera*, Signorina Mauer. I will show you to your room." He gestured to the elevators with his white-gloved hand. "*Da questa parte, per favore.*"

I started to follow then stopped and looked over my shoulder at Erudito, who'd stayed behind. He looked up from his conversation with one of the hotel staff and met my gaze. After a final word to the attendant, he joined me. "Is everything all right, signorina?" He glanced at the bellhop, who stood patiently by the elevators, then back at me.

I smiled. The man was nothing short of professional, so professional I had to wonder what he ever did for fun. "Yes, everything's fine." I paused and suddenly realized— "Oh! I should give you a tip. I'm so sorry." I rummaged in my purse for my money envelope. *Geez, how much am I supposed to tip this guy? Twenty euros? Fifty?*

Shaking his head, he waved his hand. "No, signorina. Do not feel obliged to tip. It is my pleasure and duty to assist you." He bowed his head as he tipped his hat. "Please do not hesitate to contact me if you need anything at all. *Arrivederci.* Enjoy your time here in Fiore Luna."

He left, and I stared long and hard at him until he exited the building. *No tip? Is he for real?* The man was too generous for words—and he was just the chauffeur!

I joined the bellhop at the elevators and gave him an apologetic smile. He called an elevator with a push of a button. We rode up to the forty-third floor, and my ears popped because we were so high. The doors swished open, and the plush red-carpeted hallway we stepped out onto stretched toward giant windows at each end. Soft light glowing from silver wall sconces created a cozy, serene atmosphere. The bellhop escorted me to room 4302 and opened the door.

My heart stopped. The room wasn't a suite; it was a *house*—no, a *mansion!* From the stately, elegant mahogany furniture in the living room to the giant island kitchen that looked like something straight out of one of those home-improvement shows on television, everything was sleek and classy, and it made me want to never leave. *This contest had to cost Ms. Stacson a fortune.* But then I remembered she was probably pretty well off from all of her bestselling books. The suite was probably mere pennies for her.

The bellhop gave me a short tour of the place, showing me where everything was and how things worked. We entered the master bedroom, and my jaw dropped. I couldn't get over its sheer size, which was ten times the size of my own bedroom. The giant bed looked like two king-size beds put together. The bathroom was crafted in beautiful, gleaming white marble. A basket full of bath supplies tied with a pink bow sat next to a Jacuzzi that looked big enough to fit five people. My luggage was neatly stowed on a gold shelf in the master bedroom's giant walk-in closet, and my garment bag hung from a matching gold clothes rack.

We ended the tour back at the foyer. "Signorina Mauer, is there anything else you need before I go?" the bellhop asked with a small twinkle in his eye.

I smiled, pegging the question as him wanting a tip. "No, that's all. Thank you very much." I placed a ten-euro note in his hand.

His face brightened, and he quietly slipped it into his pocket. "*Grazie.* Enjoy your stay at the Verde Suites." He tapped the brim of his hat then left.

Alone, I exhaled a huge sigh. My nerves still buzzing, I returned to the bathroom and investigated the Jacuzzi and the basket of items. I was going to make good use of those items in preparation for my night out on the town.

That evening, after a relaxing Jacuzzi bath to calm my nerves, I plopped down on the oversized bed in my nightshirt. I called Claudia from my travel cell, which I'd bought at the airport upon arriving in Bellacigna, to fill her in on my first-day adventures.

"I can't believe you're already having this much fun," Claudia said once I'd finished.

I snorted. "This is nothing compared to your meeting the *Duke* of Cittàcigni." I wondered if Erudito could introduce me to a charming duke. Or maybe even a prince?

"That was just a fluke." Claudia chuckled. "But I believe everything happens for a reason. Who knows? There may be hope for you yet to get hooked up."

"Girl, I wish. But I'm just going to enjoy every ounce of this vacation as much as I can—with or without a royal hunk."

"That's the spirit."

I'd already planned to spend some time hanging out with Claudia during my vacation. We decided on a day and time to meet up for gelato then ended the call. It was eight o'clock—we'd chatted for over an hour. I sprang out of bed, slipped on a strappy little black dress with matching open-toe heels, fixed my hair, then headed out the door.

By nine o'clock, I was standing outside a quaint hole-in-the-wall with the neon Heaven & Blues sign glowing steadily above the entrance. A brawny man in a black suit and tie stood outside the doors with his hands crossed at his waist. He looked my way, inclined his head slightly with a smile, then turned his attention to a group of girls dressed in glitzy outfits and cocktail dresses as he opened the doors for them.

"*Buonasera, signorine,*" he greeted them.

One of the girls responded in honey-toned Italian, and he let out a soft chuckle. The other girls cast flirtatious glances at him as they made their way inside. I followed the group, brushing past the doorman. I couldn't help but take a sidelong look as I passed. His enticing dark-brown eyes were practically boring holes in me. I grinned shyly at him, my cheeks getting hotter as I entered the dimly lit lounge.

The upscale, plush interior swept me away. Red-velvet sofas and chairs provided ample seating everywhere. The wait staff, dressed sharp in black suit jackets and matching bowties, glided silently between tables, carrying trays of drinks.

I claimed a small table to the left of the main stage, where a woman dressed in a long blue cocktail dress sang, accompanied by a pianist and drummer. The table's centerpiece was a red decorative glass jar, which housed a flickering tea candle that created tiny abstract designs on the white tablecloth.

Crossing my legs, I leaned an elbow on the table, my cheek cradled in my hand, and listened to the slow, mellow music. Though I couldn't understand the Italian lyrics, I still vibed out to the classic blues sound.

"*Mi scusi, signorina, vorreste da bere?*"

I blinked out of my trance and looked for the source of the solicitous male voice—an older, thin waiter with cropped salt-and-pepper hair and a matching trimmed beard. He watched me with curious eyes and an amused but charming smile. Unsure of what he was asking, I looked at him with bemusement. "Uh…"

Faint wrinkles creased his face as his smile grew. "Would you like a drink, signorina?"

A drink. I think I'm gonna need several drinks. "Oh, yes, please." My voice cracked.

The waiter looked at me expectantly.

"Ah! Um, I'll have a Pinot Grigio."

"*Ah, ottima scelta.*" He nodded, spun on his heel and headed for the bar.

Applause suddenly came from the crowd. I looked back to the stage in time to see the woman and her band take a bow. A dark curtain closed, and the lights slowly brightened. Much of the audience scattered. Some headed to the restrooms or the bar, while others made their way to the exit. But as quickly as people departed, new faces entered and took over the vacant seats.

The waiter returned with my drink, and I took a sip as the lights dimmed again, cuing the next act. The stage lights transitioned to a cool bluish color, and the curtain opened, revealing a tenor saxophone player, keyboardist, bassist, and drummer. The four men began playing a catchy jazz tune, and the low murmurs among the audience dissipated. When the band had everyone's attention, the sax player—a middle-aged man—stopped playing, and a small spotlight focused on him. While the rest of the band played at a lower volume, he spoke his introduction in Italian. I only understood his name—Vincenzo. He performed a short solo, and the rest of his band accompanied. He gave introductions to the keyboardist and bassist, Castello and Marco, and the spotlight moved to each one in turn as they gave their own solos. The drummer, Samuele, was last, and his introduction was much longer. The spotlight fixed on the man, who looked about my age, sitting behind the drum set. His short black hair was disheveled in just the right way to make my heart leap into my throat as I watched him bust out with his solo, his hands moving across the drums and cymbals with amazing dexterity and timing. Light reflected off the lenses of his black horn-rimmed glasses as he bobbed his head in time to the beat. When he finished, he looked up at the audience, a few stray locks of his hair casually falling across one side of his forehead. A shadow of beard emphasized his square jaw when he smiled. He raised his drumsticks in the air, revealing toned arms beneath the rolled-up sleeves of his plaid button-down shirt. The audience clapped, cheered, and whistled.

Well, I guess when you're that *attractive, you* deserve *massive applause.*

The band continued their set, and all I could do was stare helplessly at that drummer, barely even touching my drink. It wasn't the first time I'd fallen for a guy in a band. I'd made the terrible mistake of getting involved with the guitarist in our little blues band back in college. It hadn't ended well, and I hadn't seen him since.

Listening to the quartet playing classic jazz allowed me to momentarily forget about the bad things in the past. I bobbed my head to the rhythm of the slapping beat of the upright bass and the smooth, rolling tunes of the sax and keyboard. It took me back to my freshman year in college, when my friends and I formed a jazz-and-blues band and did little gigs around town. Claudia had even designed a cute sign for us. We spent the small tips we'd earned on ice cream to celebrate. By my late sophomore year, however, our band had broken up. Sadly, I'd lost touch with them. But that hadn't stopped me from continuing to play my electric bass. At the moment, I regretted not bringing it along.

I'd always hoped to be able to quit my barista job one day and become a full-time professional musician, traveling the world and playing to my heart's content. But I'd convinced myself that it was just a crazy fantasy.

I returned my gaze to the cute drummer, who appeared completely lost in the music. Samuele's eyes were closed, and his head moved while his hands blurred across the drums. It was almost midnight when the band ended their last set. Cheers and applause erupted from the audience, who rose to their feet. The band took a bow, and the curtain closed. The main lights came on again, signaling another intermission in preparation for the next band. Satisfied with an entertaining night, I decided to leave.

Outside, I started for the hotel, feeling physically whipped after such a long day. The jet lag didn't help, either. All I wanted was to enjoy that amazing monster-sized bed waiting for me in my suite. I stared at the line of expensive-looking cars parked along the curb near the building. There were a few more across the street. *This place must really be a hotspot for the rich and famous.*

Approaching a small alley between the lounge and another building, I heard the echo of four male voices. One of them sounded like Vincenzo. I looked toward the voices and spotted three figures illuminated in a bronze wash cast by a lone floodlight attached to a corner of one of the buildings. The men, whom I recognized as the jazz quartet from earlier, gathered near the open trunk of a dark sedan, chatting and laughing. One of the men placed a long instrument case in the trunk then slammed it shut. Samuele stood among them, with a small duffel bag slung over his shoulder.

My heart fluttered at the sight of him, even at a distance. I kept telling myself that I shouldn't be so smitten by a guy I didn't even know, and I willed my feet to continue toward the hotel. The men's voices suddenly stopped, and I glanced over my shoulder. The four of them, including Samuele, were looking in my direction.

My breath caught. *Oh, geez, now they're staring at me!* I whipped around the corner, out of their line of sight, and hugged my back to the wall of the next building. I took several deep breaths in succession, but my nerves were still rattled. Why did the mere sight of him make me act like such a high schooler? They must've all thought I was a weird groupie or something. Embarrassed, I peeled myself off the wall and walked away as quickly as my three-inch heels could take me.

Headlights shone from behind me. I didn't think much of it because of the light traffic, so I continued walking. One of the shiny, expensive cars I'd seen earlier—a white, gleaming sports car—pulled up beside me, matching my pace. I halted, and so did the car. I looked warily toward the dark-tinted window of the driver's side, but I couldn't discern anything beyond. The window slid down, and I got a good look at the driver. Time suddenly stopped.

"*Mi scusi, signorina. Si è persa?*" Samuele asked, his face filled with concern.

I simply stared at him, dumbfounded. He was apparently alone.

"Are you lost? Do you require help?" he asked again.

I blinked when he spoke in accented English. He sounded sincere enough, but my nerves were still on edge. "Oh, n-no, I'm fine. Thanks."

His head tilted slightly, and his brow furrowed. "You were at Heaven and Blues tonight, were you not?"

"Yeah, I was there. I really enjoyed your show. You're an amazing drummer."

He beamed. "*Grazie.* I am glad you enjoyed the show." He paused a beat then said, "My name is Samuele. It is a pleasure to meet you."

Hearing him utter his own name etched it into my mind. "Hi, Samuele. I'm Trina. Nice to meet you, too." I fidgeted with the strap of my purse, feeling torn because part of me said I should leave, but another part of me told me to stay and prolong the meeting just a little while longer. My rational side lost the battle when an idea suddenly came to mind. "Um, I know this is going to sound weird but..." I pulled my planner and a pen from my purse. "Can you autograph my planner?"

He gave me a funny look, probably thinking I was a serious nutcase. Maybe I was, being all starstruck like some rabid groupie. But stuff like that must happen to him all the time. I could only imagine how many women he had clamoring for his attention. Obviously, I was no better.

He adjusted his glasses, and his brow pinched. "Your... planner?"

I nodded and forced a smile, even though I was mentally kicking myself for digging my hole of shame even deeper. But I couldn't help myself. I could stare at this gorgeous Adonis forever.

I'd expected him to make a typical polite excuse that celebrities made whenever they wanted to get away from pests like me. But instead, Samuele parallel parked along the curb and got out. My legs turned to jelly, and my heart beat faster. He had a tall, lean physique and still showed off those beautifully defined forearms beneath his rolled-up shirtsleeves. When he got close, I could see the bright-emerald green of his eyes. I bit my bottom lip and showed him my Erica Collinger–brand planner that I took everywhere. I cherished the little book, with my daily life's precious schedule inscribed on its colorful sticker-and-washi-taped pages.

He looked at it for a moment then laughed. "Oh! I have a sister who is into that sort of thing. I do not understand its appeal." He took the planner and pen then signed the inside cover.

I chuckled. "Just a secret passion of mine." As he handed the planner back, I noticed on his right middle finger was a silver ring with a small crest in the inset. "Thanks for autographing it," I continued, then flipped open the cover to see what he'd written.

"*Vivere per la musica. Samuele.*" I looked back at him. "What does this mean?"

His face softened. "It means 'live for the music,' *bella.*"

A man after my own heart. "I live it all the time. Especially jazz and blues. I played with a group back in college."

"Oh? What did you play?"

"Electric bass. Fun times."

His eyebrows rose. "*Stupefacente!* I have never met a girl who plays the bass."

I blushed. "Really? Well, I guess now you can say you have."

"Do you still play?"

"Yeah, but more for myself, now. Sometimes, I miss playing with the group."

He checked his watch. "Forgive me, *bella*. I must be going now. I hope I will see you again soon."

I sighed. *Of course he has to go. Other obligations, like perhaps a significant other.* "Yeah… I guess I shouldn't hold you up any more. I'd love to check out more of your upcoming gigs, though."

He flashed a warm and bright smile that could melt ice cream. "That would be great. I will be at *Due Passi Salotto* in Cittàcigni this Friday, at eight o'clock."

A quick check of my planner showed that time slot was empty—thank goodness. Most of my sightseeing was planned during the day. He gave me the details, and I quickly jotted down the information. "Thanks. I'll be there."

Samuele's concern returned to his face. "Do you need a lift?"

I sank my teeth into my bottom lip, tempted to say yes, but my rational, cautious side won the battle this time. With a small, disappointed sigh, I shook my head. "Thank you, but there's no need. I'm staying at Verde Suites just down the street." I pointed.

"Okay. Be safe, then, *bella*. I will look for you on Friday night. *Ciao*." He returned to his car.

I waited for him to leave first, but when he didn't, I started toward the hotel. He turned his headlights on, creating an illuminated path all the way down the street. I occasionally looked over my shoulder and noticed he still hadn't budged from his parking spot. I was only a few yards away from the hotel's entrance when the light faded. I turned again, to wave at him and let him know I was okay, but he was already gone.

CHAPTER 2

I WAS STILL SLEEPY FROM THE JET LAG WHEN I got up early on Tuesday. But as the morning went on, my body adjusted, and by eight o'clock, I was fully awake to tour the *Teatro all Diamante* and Fiore Luna Cathedral. Both gothic structures took my breath away. My last stop was the Rose Symphony Music Hall. The centuries-old building was still a famous venue that hosted many bands and musical artists from all over the world. I wondered if Samuele ever played there.

By noon, I'd finished the day's sightseeing and returned to my suite to get ready for my visit to M.E. Stacson. I had brought along one of my favorite outfits for the occasion. While I was getting dressed, my phone buzzed on the nightstand. The screen displayed Claudia's number, and I smiled. "Hey, you."

"Hey, Trina. Back from sightseeing yet?"

"Yep, just got back not long ago. I would love to attend a show or service at the city's famous theater and cathedral just to experience their ambience."

"Yeah, a lot of the Bellacignan towns have hidden gems like them."

I yawned. "I just wish this jet lag would stop kicking my butt. You realize I'm supposed to still be asleep around this time back home?"

Claudia chuckled. "It's annoying in the beginning, but then you start to get used to it."

"By the time I get used to it, I'll be heading back to South Carolina." I rolled my eyes.

"Hey, Stefano and I are on our way to a benefit concert in Alta Rosa. Want to join us for a late lunch or gelato afterward?

I wanted to reply with an enthusiastic yes, but I had my own schedule. "I can't. I'm supposed to meet M.E. Stacson for lunch in two hours. But that gelato date is still on for Friday."

"Definitely!"

We ended the call, and I stared at Claudia's number, eager to finally see her. But since marrying Stefano, she was nothing short of busy, which mostly consisted of community service. Being a duke's wife certainly had its perks, but it also had many responsibilities. I couldn't imagine myself in Claudia's shoes. But despite it all, she was happy, and that was all I ever wanted for my best friend.

Leaving the hotel, I spotted Erudito leaning against the hood of a fancy black sedan parked out front. I had no idea how long he'd been waiting, but he obviously hadn't forgotten about my meeting with M.E. Stacson. His head was down while he studied something on his cell phone. As I came closer, he looked up at me and stuffed the phone into his blazer. Smiling, he pushed himself off the sedan and opened the back passenger door.

"*Buon pomeriggio,* Signorina Mauer," he greeted.

"Hi, Erudito," I said in a bubbly tone, then settled into the backseat.

He smiled, shut the door, and climbed into the driver's seat. "Signora Stacson cannot wait to meet you."

My heart pounded. In just a few minutes, I would be meeting a famous international bestselling author. *My* favorite author. And she wanted to meet *me*!

As we drove through town, I stared out the window. We passed the Heaven and Blues lounge, and memories of the previous night sparked in my brain. Memories of Samuele. I took out my planner from my purse and stared at his signature on the inside front cover. Gently tracing my fingers across the scrawled black lettering, I whispered, *"Vivere per la musica…"*

We stopped at a stoplight, and a cozy yet rustic-looking building on the street corner drew my eye. A small, thin wooden sign that said *"Dolce Sinfonia Negozio di Musica"* swung lightly beneath the blue-and-white shop awning. Through the large glass windows, I spotted guitars hanging on racks, amplifiers, keyboards, and more. I sighed—I hadn't stepped into a music store since our group disbanded.

We left the city's outskirts and drove through a picturesque countryside, where acres of vineyards and farmlands dotted the landscape. Erudito turned off the main road and down a narrow gravel path that was secluded by a canopy of flowering ivy that hung from a long, arched trellis. Even from inside the car,

I could smell honeysuckle, jasmine, and moonflower. We drove for several minutes through the tunnel of pleasant-smelling flora before finally emerging into a clearing, where a giant Italian-style villa sat.

My mouth dropped open, and I stared wide-eyed at the castle-sized home. "This… this is M.E. Stacson's house?" I asked breathlessly.

"Sì," Erudito replied. He drove along an arched cobblestone driveway and parked the sedan before a shallow set of stairs leading up to the front entrance, which was decorated by tall, white columns on either side. Vines wrapped around the columns and curled along the brickwork of the villa, creating a classic Renaissance-style look. Erudito left the driver's seat and opened the door for me.

My feet were like concrete. I'd never seen a house this big in person. *Was this how Claudia felt when she first visited Stefano's house?*

"Are you all right, signorina?" Erudito asked, concern filling his deep voice.

I tore my gaze from the house and looked up at him. "I-I'm fine. Sorry, I was just thinking." I took his extended hand.

Smiling, he helped me out of the car. I smoothed out the small wrinkles in my floral sundress and checked the straps of my yellow sandals before following him to the entrance. We didn't get far up the stairs before the door opened suddenly and an older woman in a black-and-white maid's outfit stood in the doorway.

"*Salve!*" she greeted us with a wave. She and Erudito had a brief exchange in Italian, then the woman looked at me and gestured with a tilt of her head. "This way, signorina."

Erudito remained in the entryway. I looked at him, wondering if he was joining us, but I received my silent answer when he urged me with a nod to follow the maid. Afterward, he left. I followed the maid through a giant room that looked like a library. Lining the white walls were tall bookshelves that stretched as high as the arched ceiling. Hundreds, perhaps thousands of titles ranged from Dante and Hemmingway to Stephen King. I also noted some of M.E. Stacson's books among them. I was seriously in heaven. *I wonder if she's read all these books?*

We snaked through many more rooms and finally emerged into a courtyard that was half the size of a football field. A large marble fountain sat in the middle, shooting spray in various patterns from majestic swan and dolphin statues. Beyond the fountain was a swimming pool with a rock waterfall. Sweet-smelling moonflower ivy dangled from wooden trellises that lined the sitting area. This magical place felt so peaceful and serene, I could've lived here forever. I followed the maid toward the sitting area, which consisted of a fancy velvet chaise lounge and a small wrought-iron dinette for two.

A dark-haired woman with bright-green eyes sat at the dinette, which was covered with colorful sticker sheets, pens, and washi tape. I slowed my walk. My heart pounded. Her black-and-white photos on the backs of all her books didn't do her justice. She looked older than twenty-three but still every bit as beautiful. I watched her taut face as she carefully laid stickers and tape down in a spiral-bound book. *Oh, my goodness. She's a planner geek, too!*

The maid nudged me forward. My foot made a sliding sound as it dragged along the stone walkway. Ms. Stacson looked up and grinned.

Behind me, the maid gave a small curtsy. "*Altezza Reale, questa è Signorina* Trina Mauer, *l'appuntamento dall'America.*"

Hearing my name among the string of mostly unfamiliar Italian phrases, I smiled in greeting. "Hello, Ms. Stacson. It's such an honor to meet you."

Ms. Stacson's face softened, and she stood. She was thin and about two inches shorter than I was. "Ah, *meraviglioso!* I am so happy to have you here, Signorina Mauer. Please, you may call me Adelina." She gestured to the other vacant chair.

Adelina? I furrowed my brow, wondering how she derived the "M.E." initials in her pen name.

As I sat, Adelina dismissed the maid and seated herself. I scooted to the edge of my chair, ogling the woman across from me and her beautiful home. If I were an author, I would never run out of ideas in such a place. No wonder Adelina continuously wrote four books a year—four *bestselling* books a year.

"I can't believe… I'm here right now," I stammered. "With you. I mean…"

She simply watched me, smiling. I sensed a hint of amusement in her eyes.

"You're like… my most favorite author of all time," I continued. "Oh my gosh, did you know we're the same age and almost have the same birthday? Mine is July seventeenth—a week after yours! I mean, we could've been sisters in another lifetime, y'know?"

She clapped her hands together. "*Eccellente*! Well, it is fortunate that it was you who won the contest. You have my congratulations and thanks for participating."

"To be honest, I didn't think I'd win. I mean, I never win anything, y'know?"

She laughed. "My *nonna* used to say, 'Good fortune tends to find us when we least expect it.'"

"And I think the coolest thing of all is that you're into your planner as much as I am." I gestured to the colorful supplies on the table. "You have *got* to tell me where you buy your stuff. Mine is in need of some love for next month." I plunked my planner down on the table.

Her eyes widened. "Oh, I *love* Erica Collinger. But I prefer bullet journaling."

We chatted for several minutes about our planners, and Adelina gave me a long list of online shops where she bought her decorating supplies. This was truly the happiest day of my life.

The maid returned with lunch. I helped Adelina clear the table of the planner decorations, then the maid set down a big, rectangular plate of something she called *insalata caprese*, which looked like nothing more than tomatoes topped with slices of fresh mozzarella and basil. Though it looked so simple, it tasted great. Adelina and I chatted more while we ate, with me asking her a thousand and one questions about her books. Though she didn't go into much detail about her personal life, it was still quite uplifting to hear of her struggles to fame.

"Wow, rejected ninety-eight times?" I blinked. "But your romance novels are so good!"

She cut a slice of cheese-and-basil-topped tomato with her fork and nibbled on it daintily. "Well, apparently they were not good enough to sell to agents and some publishers. I was hoping to make it to a hundred rejections so I could celebrate."

I raised my eyebrows. "Why would you want to celebrate a hundred failures?"

"To me, rejections are not failures. They are merely stepping stones to reach your goal. And behold, one day, a friend of the family who owns Editori Bellacigna, one of the largest international publishing companies in Europe, happened upon my manuscript, *Cielo Azzurro oltre Bellacigna*—Blue Skies over Bellacigna—and decided to give it a chance. Just four days after the book was published, it reached number-one spots on all major bestseller lists." She grinned.

"It was well deserved. I've read that book a hundred times. Such an amazing story."

"*Grazie.*" She inclined her head.

With the last of the appetizer eaten, the maid returned and cleared away the plates. Then she set down a rotini main course and poured us both glasses of homemade *limoncello*. The wine had a strong lemony taste but wasn't too bitter.

"Do you really live in this huge house all alone?" I asked.

Adelina swirled her wine glass between her slender, perfectly manicured fingers. "Not entirely alone. Erudito makes great company sometimes."

He sure does, I thought, smiling at the mention of the charming chauffeur.

"He works entirely too hard," Adelina continued. "I wish he would take a break sometime. I would have preferred Salvo, my parents' chauffeur, to pick you up from the airport, instead, but Erudito insisted on doing it. I feel bad burdening him with so many tasks and responsibilities."

"Maybe he likes his job," I said. "He seems to, anyway. I mean, he didn't even want a tip."

Adelina chewed a modest forkful of rotini. "Sì, he does not like accepting tips. I still do not know why. It is strange, but he is quite content, nonetheless."

We finished the rest of the delicious lunch, then the maid cleared away the plates and offered us shots of espresso. Not used to drinking espresso from such a tiny cup, I downed the contents in one go.

"During your stay in Bellacigna, you should make time to visit Alta Rosa, the capital city, and meet the king and queen."

I sighed. "I'd love to meet them. My best friend, Claudia, got herself snagged by a handsome Bellacignan duke."

Adelina's brow furrowed. "You do not mean Claudia Trevisani, do you?"

"The very one." I grinned. "She married Stefano, the Duke of Cittàcigni, last year."

She looked thoughtful for a moment. Then her face softened. She leaned in closer and said in a quieter voice, "I will share a secret with you, since you are Claudia's best friend."

Always loving a good secret, I leaned in eagerly.

"Stefano Trevisani is my cousin. I was so happy when I heard that he finally married and took his place as the new duke. Claudia is a lovely woman, and they are so very much in love with each other."

My jaw dropped. *My favorite author in the world is related to the Trevisani family? To my best friend's husband? This is surreal.* "A-Are you serious?" I stammered, wide-eyed. "D-Does that mean you're a duchess or something?"

She averted her gaze. "Ah, not exactly."

"Wow, I would've never guessed you were related to the royal family. So why do you write under a pen name?"

She fell silent for a moment then looked back at me. "I enjoy its mysteriousness."

I chuckled. "Okay, well, your secret is safe with me. I promise."

"*Grazie.*" She pulled back a ruffled sleeve of her purple blouse, revealing a diamond-studded watch, and raised her eyebrows. "*Oddio!* It is almost four o'clock! I am sure you would like to do some touring and whatnot before evening." She stood. "Forgive me for keeping you here for so long."

I stood as well. "What? No, this was the best day ever, spending time talking with my favorite author. It's been a great honor. I hope we can do this again real soon."

"Sì, we can whenever you wish. Just give Erudito a call." She picked up a cell phone that sat atop her closed notebook and called Erudito. The hunky chauffeur strolled into the courtyard minutes later, and after I said my goodbyes to Adelina, he escorted me to the exit.

I climbed into the backseat of the car, and Erudito shut the door. I stared out the window at the villa's massive and intriguing entrance one last time. As we pulled away, my face remained glued to the window. We drove along the gravel path and beneath the arched trellis tunnel of hanging ivy, where the sight of the luxurious home disappeared behind the veil of fragrant flora.

Within twenty minutes, we were back in Fiore Luna's city limits. The sights of the familiar buildings and shops as we trekked the same route back to the hotel reminded me of the sight-seeing tour and trip to the museum I had planned for the next day.

We stopped at a stoplight, and my eyes cut to the wooden *Dolce Sinfonia Negozio di Musica* store sign, swinging slowly back and forth in the breeze. I'd blocked out the rest of the day for my visit with M.E. Stacson, but since that was done, I had a free schedule. I figured I could take a quick peek in that music store then call Claudia to see if she was still in town. Maybe I could take her up on that gelato offer a few days early.

I leaned forward between the two front seats. "Hey, Erudito. Can you drop me off here?"

He turned his head slightly toward me and arched an eyebrow. "Right here, signorina?"

"Yes, I want to visit that music store across the street. And maybe get a gelato. Besides, the hotel is just a few blocks away. I don't mind walking. It's such a nice day."

He smiled at that. "*Ma certo.* There is a good *gelateria* just that way." He pointed down a side street, which had more little shops.

I followed his direction and nodded, taking note. "Great."

Erudito parked along the curb and got out. He opened my door, and I climbed out, garnering a few glances from passersby along the sidewalk.

"Thank you," I said to Erudito, ignoring the stares.

"*Prego.* Please contact me if you need my service again."

The sincerity of his voice made me smile. "I will, thanks. See you later."

"*Arrivederci.*" He tipped his hat then returned to the driver's side. After casting another quick glance at me, he got in and drove off. I watched him until the shiny black sedan disappeared in the sea of traffic along the main street.

I crossed the busy street to the music store and peered through one of the windows at the various instruments on display. I didn't notice anyone walking around inside and wondered if the place was closed already. According to the sign on the window, the store didn't close until five o'clock. I tried the wooden door, and it swung open. Relief spread through me as a set of bells over the door jingled cheerily. As I entered, I heard the sound of light piano music playing in the back of the store. The front door closed behind me, and the piano music stopped suddenly. I wandered through the store, instinctively drawn toward the guitars and basses in one corner. I admired the designer ones with hefty price tags hanging on the wall. *But oh, wouldn't it be fun to play them all!*

A gold-trimmed, black-and-purple fretless bass on display caught my attention. It was a replica—or perhaps the actual one—that my musical idol, Daisy Weatherspoon, played at all her concerts. She'd dyed her short, cropped hair purple to match, which garnered her nickname by her fans "Purple Daisy." She'd also given her bass the same name. The eight-thousand-euro price tag attached to the instrument made me nearly choke on my breath.

"*Salve, signora. Come posso aiutarti?*"

I started at the voice behind me then spun around. There stood a tall, athletically built man with short, slicked-back dark hair and olive skin. His dark-brown eyes looked at me with such interest, it made me blush. Then I recognized him as the bassist from Erudito's band.

"H-Hi…" I said in a short breath. My gaze dropped a moment to his gold-plated nametag that said "Marco," which confirmed my suspicions.

He grinned and said in heavily accented English, "Hi. Are you looking for something in particular?"

Focusing on his face again, I swallowed then licked my drying lips. "Ah, n-not really. Just browsing."

He gestured to the basses on the wall. "You play?"

I wrung my hands and averted my gaze to a more plain-looking jazz bass with a more reasonable price tag, sitting on a stand nearby. "A little," I muttered.

He walked into my line of sight, retrieved the instrument from the stand, and handed it to me. "Try it and see what you think."

I blinked and looked at him in disbelief. "I'm allowed?"

"*Certo*, signorina. You may try them all, if you wish."

Of course, I would have *loved* to try the purple fretless, but the thought of so much as breathing on the thing made my stomach knot. But the one Marco handed me felt a lot like my own. I sat on a small padded stool and plugged the bass into an amplifier sitting next to it. Marco watched me get situated then turned on the amplifier for me.

I strummed a few strings, producing a full sound that resonated from the amp. *Beautiful.* The bass sounded a lot like mine. *Must be a similar brand or something.* I played a few chords and riffs from some of the songs I used to play with my band. Then I began playing "A Fairytale Kind of Love," one of Daisy Weatherspoon's hit songs that I knew like the back of my hand. Marco watched silently, his eyes twinkling with slight intrigue.

I strummed the last note and let it fade on its own.

Marco raised his eyebrows. "That did not sound like you play 'a little.'" He chuckled.

I scratched the back of my head as I tried to fight down a smile. "Okay, well maybe I might've played *a little* jazz back in college."

Smirking, he grabbed a red-and-black electric guitar off another rack and plugged it in to another amplifier. His fingers raced across the six strings in an eye-popping dexterous display as he rocked out on a snazzy riff. He ended on the final note and looked back at me coyly.

I knew a challenge when I heard one. Grinning, I responded with a fast slap style that got my fingers working up and down the neck. I hadn't played that aggressively in years. I'd forgotten how fun it was.

We still had the store to ourselves, so we continued our little back-and-forth game until my fingers felt as if they were about to fall off.

"You are good, signorina," Marco said, laughing.

I joined in his laughter. "Thanks. So are you. What other instruments do you play?"

"Guitar and bass, mainly. But Castello is teaching me a little keyboard, too."

"Wow. Multitalented. My name is Trina, by the way."

"*Hai un nome bellissima.*" He strummed a chord on his guitar. "I am Marco."

"Yeah, I figured from your nametag." I gave him a sly grin. "And I saw you play at Heaven and Blues last night."

"Oh?" He continued playing. "Were you there? We had a lively crowd."

"Yeah, you guys were amazing." *Especially the drummer.* My heart pounded as thoughts of Samuele crossed my mind.

"*Grazie.* I am glad you enjoyed the show." Marco tapped his foot steadily then started into a random jazzy tune.

I couldn't help but join in. I complemented his style with my own, strumming chords and enhancing the song in time to the beat. We exchanged smiles as we jammed out right there in the store. It had been a long time since I'd had so much fun. Minutes later, we wrapped up the song and took a break.

"That was great!" I said, stretching my fingers.

Marco rose, unplugged the guitar, and returned it to its stand. "You are not so bad yourself, *bella.*"

The bells at the entrance rang, indicating a new customer. I craned my neck to see who it was, but the sea of instruments on display blocked my view. Marco looked toward the sound then back at me. "*Un momento.*" He hurried to the front of the store and disappeared.

As I unplugged the wire from the bass, my phone buzzed in my purse. I checked it. Claudia had texted, asking me to call her tonight. I glanced at the time on the lit-up screen and realized it was nearing five o'clock in the evening. The music store would be closing soon. I'd sated my desires long enough, and it was time I returned to the hotel and filled Claudia in on Day Two of my Bellacignan adventure.

I headed for the entrance. My gaze flicked toward the front counter, where Marco and the new customer, another man, who had his back to me, were chatting. Marco stopped talking and looked up at me.

"Ah! *Addio*, signorina!" he called, waving.

I waved back.

The other man looked over his shoulder, and the light briefly reflected off the lenses of his glasses. His face softened.

Samuele. My breath hitched. I grabbed the handle of the front door but couldn't muster the strength or willpower to leave, not when that cute drummer guy was staring back at me.

Samuele faced me and smiled. "So we meet again, *bella.*"

So we do. I swallowed, unable to form coherent words to speak.

Samuele turned again, said something to Marco, then started walking in my direction, carrying two little packets containing drum damper pads and cymbal felts.

Oh geez. Here he comes…

He reached the door I was currently blocking and slowly scanned me up and down, burning my skin.

"H-Hi, Samuele…" I said in almost a whisper.

His eyes narrowed in amusement. "Hi. Marco told me you are pretty good on the bass."

My cheeks got ten degrees hotter. I glanced in Marco's direction, and he smirked. "Oh, I… I play here and there," I said, looking back at Samuele. I suddenly realized I was still blocking the exit, so I quickly stood aside so that he could leave.

"We should jam sometime." Samuele held open the door, his gaze fixed on me. "Are you leaving, signorina?"

Of course I was. But he'd just invited me to jam with him. My brain was still processing the possibilities with Samuele while my body was wrestling with the present. *C'mon, Trina! Stop standing there, looking like a fool.* I took a deep breath. "Ah, yeah. I was just on my way to the hotel." I finally managed to will my feet to move. After waving another goodbye to Marco, I joined Samuele outside.

A black stretch limo sat along the curb, and a chauffeur stood next to the vehicle, his hands folded in front of him while he waited patiently. He spotted Samuele and tipped his black hat.

I raised my eyebrows at Samuele. "Wow, riding fancy today, I see."

He chuckled. "Sì. I had to play at a benefit concert today."

I blinked. *Benefit concert?* Was it the same one that Claudia and Stefano had gone to? "There's no better way to travel than in style," was all I could say.

He laughed. "Sì, but I would have preferred to just drive myself or take a taxi." He walked toward the back passenger side, and the chauffeur opened the door. Before climbing in, Samuele looked over his shoulder at me. "Are you still coming to the gig on Friday?"

He still remembered. I nodded. "I wouldn't miss it for the world."

"*Ottimo.* I will see you then." He got in the limo, and the chauffeur shut the door.

I watched the limo speed off. *Friday can't come soon enough.* Maybe in addition to gelato, Claudia and I could make it a full-blown girls' night out on Friday. It would be fun to not only swoon over Samuele onstage but also spend some quality girl time with my best friend.

CHAPTER 3

CLAUDIA AND I PULLED AN ALL-NIGHTER, chatting nonstop on the phone. It reminded me of our early college days when we'd literally talked until the sun came up. Sleep was the last thing on our minds whenever cute guys were the subject of our conversation.

I'd been dreaming nonstop of Samuele as I eagerly anticipated his gig on Friday. I thought about returning to the music store in hopes of bumping into him again, but my Wednesday and Thursday were fully planned with more sightseeing tours and visits to the museum, the library, the city's famous giant rose garden at the *Parco Giardino Verde Smeraldo*, as well as a carriage ride through some of Bellacigna's historic countryside, a hiking trip in the mountains, a river cruise, and a trip to some of the many vineyards.

The Bellacignan culture was intriguing, heavily bred on Italian culture. Learning more about the cities and towns that made up this small country was like listening to a fairy tale. Stories of royalty and happily-ever-afters made it seem worlds apart from my life back home.

Thursday night, I returned to my hotel after a long day of excitement and souvenir shopping and plopped into bed. I closed my eyes and immediately fell asleep. Even though I hadn't seen Samuele for two days, he remained on my mind.

I woke on Friday, ready for my date with Claudia, who was going to show me the University of Cittàcigni, where she worked as an art teacher. Fiore Luna's train station was a short walk away, and the ride to Cittàcigni was only fifteen minutes. Never having been on such a fast train before, I ogled at the sight of the beautiful country whooshing past my window. Around noon, the train arrived at the Cittàcigni station. I followed the crowd through the building, which was made up in white marble and majestic fountains and statues of swans throughout.

I made my way outside, where a line of taxis and expensive cars waited along the curb. I immediately spotted Claudia standing next to a cherry-red convertible. No one would've ever thought she was a duke's wife, as she wore a plain-looking green sundress and matching green flats, no crazy makeup or sparkly jewelry. Our eyes finally met, and her smooth, sandy-brown face lit up.

We both ran to each other and crashed into each other's arms in a tight embrace.

"Look at you, Miss Bellacignan Duchess!" I exclaimed after we pulled away.

Claudia chuckled. "I'm still not quite sure of my title. But I think I just like being considered Stefano's wife."

I caught glimpses of some of the people around us who stared curiously at the commotion we were causing. A few people smiled at Claudia as if they recognized her. My heart wouldn't stop thumping with excitement. Claudia still looked and acted the same as she had when I saw her last year. She would always be my best friend and the sister I never had.

"Where is Stefano, anyway?" I asked, craning my neck and looking around.

"He had some speaking engagements to do at the college." Claudia opened the passenger door for me.

I looked at the open door a moment then furrowed my brow. "And since when is the duchess also a chauffeur?"

"I'm not a chauffeur. Stefano was going to send one out to get you, but I managed to talk him into letting me pick you up instead. I wanted to see you again so bad."

I laughed.

"And stop calling me 'duchess.' I'm still Claudia to you."

I got in the car, and Claudia took the wheel. It still caught me by surprise, as I'd expected an actual chauffeur to be driving the new duchess around. It only confirmed that beneath the fancy title, Claudia was still the same girl from college. During our sophomore year, Claudia had been the only one with a car, so she often drove us around.

Cittàcigni was as beautiful as Claudia had described. It reminded me a lot of Fiore Luna, only instead of a rose theme that enchanted the city, there were swans. From the statues to murals and even actual live swans that swam through the park lake, everything about the place was touched with a fairy-tale feel. It was a colorful city, and I could definitely see someone like Claudia getting artistic inspiration from it. We arrived at the University of Cittàcigni's tree-lined campus, which looked about as big as the University of South Carolina. We drove through campus and into a parking garage next to the Art and Music building. Compared to the rest of the ivy-covered brick buildings that carried a charm from the Italian Renaissance, the newly built Art and Music building was colorful, geometric, and chic. Claudia parked in a reserved space that had her name written on it, along with a matching sign placed in front.

"Wow, your space is right next to Paul Lessaire?" I asked, pointing to the famous interior designer's name stenciled on the adjacent space.

"Yeah, isn't it great? Paul is such a gentleman. He teaches the upper-level art theory class. I usually see him every morning before classes start."

My mouth dropped open. "I am *so* jealous of you right now."

I followed Claudia inside the main building while she rapped out interesting facts about the college. The interior was just as intricate and next-gen as the exterior. Oddly shaped windows containing stained-glass murals filtered the sunlight through the halls in a brilliant, colorful display. Tapestries and paintings hung from the ivory walls, and glass displays holding various artistic antiquities dotted the halls. This place reminded me of a museum, but it seemed like a true artist's dream. I certainly understood why Claudia felt at home there.

On our way to Claudia's office, we passed students, mostly young, but some old. Some stopped to say hi to Claudia, while others were in such a hurry, they whooshed past us. It seemed the college environment in Bellacigna wasn't so different from the one back home.

We entered a door, which led to the faculty area, and walked to the end of the hall to Claudia's office. She opened her door to a small but quaint room that contained her personal touches, like her own art pieces hanging on the wall and her "cute cat artist" stuffed animal I'd sent her last year. I immediately claimed a comfortable-looking black couch sitting across from her desk. I sank down on the soft leather with a sigh and kicked off my shoes.

"Oh, that feels great," I said, wiggling my toes.

Claudia laughed. "Oh c'mon, girl. Your feet should be used to walking around USC's campus for four years."

"Yeah, I wore sneakers back then, not sandals with heels." I glanced around the room. "This is a neat little office. I can't believe you have your own."

"It's really all Stefano's doing. He insisted that I have my own office. All the pampering can get overwhelming sometimes, but he only means well."

What I wouldn't have given to have a handsome Bellacignan guy pamper me to no end. "So we've really got the whole day to ourselves?"

She shook her head. "Not quite. I have one class to teach in about an hour, but after that, it will be just you and me."

I grinned. "Sounds great, because I'm craving some gelato."

"Me, too." She sighed. "Tomorrow's going to be so busy preparing for that ball."

I blinked. "A ball? As in a royal ball? Like the ones in the fairy tales?"

"It's more like a gathering of family and friends. The Trevisani family put one on every year. I totally would have invited you if I'd known you'd win a trip to Bellacigna two months later. But the attendee roster has been finalized, and they are not doing any amendments." She frowned. "I really wish you could come. Maybe I can talk to Stefano about—"

"No, don't worry about it. We'll have plenty of other opportunities to hang out before I leave."

Her lips tugged with a small smile. "Thanks for understanding, Trina. Say, how would you like to sit in on one of my classes? See me in action?"

"Am I allowed? I mean…"

"Of course you are. You're my friend, and it's *my* class." She rolled the chair from behind the desk over to me, turned it backwards, and sat down straddling it, resting her arms along the back. "I really missed you, Trina."

"I missed you, too. Told you we'd see each other again soon. I was thinking, in addition to gelato, let's go out for drinks tonight. Samuele has a gig at the *Due Passi Salotto*, and—"

Claudia's face lit up. "That would be perfect! I'd love to meet Samuele. Let's make it a girls' night out tonight."

I raised my eyebrows. "You sure Stefano won't mind if I steal you away tonight?"

"Nah, he'll be fine."

A knock suddenly came from the door, followed by a voice. "*Ci sei, bella?*"

Claudia beamed. "Speaking of whom…" She got up from the chair and answered the door. The six-foot-something handsome Bellacignan duke with short, dark curly hair, olive skin, and a charming smile stepped inside. He was dressed in a suit and tie and had a manila envelope tucked under one arm— so professional, so adorable. Nothing like the deejay pictures I'd seen of him on the Internet.

My feet miraculously stopped aching in that moment as I sprang up from the couch. "Y-Your Majesty—"

Claudia giggled. "No, Trina. He's not a king. You're supposed to address him as 'Your Grace.'"

"Oh, sorry. Your Grace." Blushing, I scratched the back of my head.

Claudia turned to Stefano. "Stefano, this is my best friend, Trina."

"*Ciao*, Trina." Stefano took my hand in his and kissed the top.

"H-Hi," I said breathlessly, relishing his soft touch.

He looked at me deeply. His emerald-green eyes were unmistakable. Something about them looked familiar. But maybe I was just so much in awe of all the cute Bellacignan guys that it was all a blur of beauty.

"I bid you a formal welcome to Bellacigna and to Cittàcigni," Stefano said, letting go of my hand. "Claudia mentioned you are here because you won a contest?"

My nerves starting to feel less rattled, I managed to reply more coherently, "Yeah. It was hosted by my favorite romance author, Adel—ah, M.E. Stacson."

His brow pinched a moment, then he nodded and turned to Claudia. "Claudia, I just stopped by briefly to give you this." He presented the manila envelope.

She took it from him and peered inside. Her face lit up. "Oh, this is wonderful. So many sign-ups!" She set the envelope on the desk. "This art show is going to be a success."

"*Naturalmente sarà!* It was your idea, *bella.*"

"Okay, I'll look this over in full later. Right now, Claudia and I have got some planning to do for our girls' night out, so shoo." She flicked her wrist at him playfully.

Stefano gave her an amused smile. "Oh, fine. I know when I am not wanted. Where are you two going, anyway?"

Claudia raised her eyebrows. "Why? Are you planning on stalking us?"

He shook his head. "No, I promise, I will not stalk you. I was just curious, that is all."

"It's the *Due Passi Salotto*. Now remember your promise."

"I promise." He opened the door.

"I'm so excited about seeing Samuele play those drums again, girl, you just don't know," I muttered.

Claudia looked over her shoulder and grinned. "And I'm sure he'll be just as excited about seeing you, too."

Stefano paused, his hand falling away from the door handle. He turned to me, his brow furrowed. "Samuele? Drummer? Did I hear that correctly?"

I nodded. "Yeah, he plays drums for a jazz band. Really talented." *And really cute.*

His face brightened. "If that is who I think it is, then please tell him I said 'hi' if you see him, okay?"

I looked at Claudia, confused and mind-boggled. She returned the stare, and that silent question was asked between us. *Does he really know Samuele?*

"Wait. How do you know Samuele?" she asked Stefano.

"Samuele Trevisani is my cousin. I always remembered him playing the drums since he was a child. He was really good. Always loved putting on a show for the kids. He played at the benefit concert the other day."

"What! I had no idea that was him!" Claudia stared openmouthed. "Why didn't you tell me?"

He shrugged. "You did not ask. Besides, how did I know you and your friend were fond of him?"

Claudia looked as though she were about to speak then closed her mouth. She looked at me hopelessly.

All I could do was stare, wondering if my ears were deceiving me or if Samuele really was a Bellacignan royal in disguise. Stefano left and shut the door behind him. The office was deathly quiet until suddenly, Claudia and I fell into a squealing fit.

"Stefano's cousin! Can you believe it?" I said.

Claudia shook her head. "It's crazy, I'll tell you what. I've been married to Stefano for a year, and I have yet to meet all of the Trevisanis. They are a *huge* family."

My cheeks hurt from smiling so much. Perhaps my wishes of getting swept up in the arms of a handsome Bellacignan duke weren't so far off after all. Maybe I would find my happily ever after, just like Claudia.

An hour later, I was sitting in the back of Claudia's full art class, which was set in an auditorium classroom with stadium-style seating. Claudia looked confident in her craft as she stood at the podium all alone, teaching about basic sketching techniques. Unlike her fully engaged students, I was distracted by the thought of seeing Samuele and realizing he had more secrets than he'd initially let on.

CHAPTER 4

FRIDAY NIGHT, CLAUDIA AND I ARRIVED VIA limo at *Due Passi Salotto* about thirty minutes after it had opened. Unlike the posh style of Heaven and Blues, *Due Passi Salotto* was tiny and had a low-lit, industrial-style interior. Exposed silver air-conditioning ducts snaked along the open ceiling. Vintage jazz posters and vinyl records were plastered haphazardly on the light-blue walls. The place was filling up fast, with only few empty tables left. We claimed a table to the side of the stage, which was a small platform raised a foot from the ground.

Currently performing on stage were two women, one on the grand piano and another on a tenor saxophone.

A waiter came to take our drink orders then disappeared. Leaning her elbows on the table, Claudia looked around with a dreamy expression.

"You ever think about playing in a band again?" she asked me. "Maybe even doing it for a living?"

Many times, I thought. But I doubted I was good enough to make a comfortable living. Acquiring gigs had been hard back in college, and sometimes, schedules would suddenly fall through. Each day was a gamble. I couldn't live like that. "Not really," I finally said. "It was fun in college, but I need a more stable job, y'know?"

"Ever thought about teaching at the university? Stefano's new art and music program has gone viral. The school is hiring more instructors."

I shook my head. "I don't think that's for me."

The waiter returned with our drinks. Before Claudia could indulge in her rosy-pink Moscato, her cell phone vibrated in her purse. She fished out the phone. One quick glance at the lit-up screen, and she chuckled. "Oh, Stefano's so crazy."

I quirked an eyebrow. "What did he say?"

Smirking, Claudia showed me the text, which was a selfie of Stefano in an oversized shirt, jeans, and a backward baseball cap. He made a funny face as he held a red rose between his teeth. Beneath the picture was a text that said: *"Manca la mia bella."*

"What does it say?" I furrowed my brow at the unfamiliar Italian.

"It says he's missing me. He has to work at one of the clubs tonight."

"Wow, you can read and understand Italian already?"

She shrugged. "I'm not fluent at it, but I'm getting there slowly. I only know a few phrases here and there."

"Wow, you go, girl."

The lights in the club began to slowly dim. The place was packed. Not a single seat available. Four men's silhouettes walked onstage, taking their places behind their respective instruments. A dim spotlight shone down on them, and my heart pounded.

Claudia nudged my arm. "Is that him?"

I stared at the man behind the drums. It was him all right. And he was every bit as handsome as the last time I saw him.

"I guess that answers my question," Claudia said again, amusement in her voice. "He is kinda cute. Hope he plays as good as he looks."

Oh, you have no idea.

Marco, on his guitar, smiled charmingly at the audience while Vincenzo did the band's introduction. Samuele looked my way, and our gazes locked. My cheeks hurt from blushing and smiling so much. At the end of his introduction, Samuele raised his drumsticks in the air, and the audience cheered extra loud for him.

He seems like the most popular one of the bunch. I wonder if other people know he's a Trevisani. I took a long sip of Pinot Grigio, while Claudia nursed her Moscato.

The band played various jazz and blues songs throughout the night. The audience was on the edge of their seats for the entire set. Even Claudia and I barely talked while they performed. Around eleven thirty, the last song finished, and the band took a bow to the audience's standing ovation. The band waved before hurriedly packing up their things and heading off the stage. Another small band was scheduled to go on next, but I wasn't at all interested.

Samuele's band walked past our table. Marco looked my way and smiled. I blushed and tried to avert my eyes. But my wandering gaze suddenly landed on Samuele, who hung back and stopped at our table, holding his drumsticks in one hand. My attention remained fixed on him until Claudia elbowed me in the arm, breaking me out of my trance.

"H-Hi, Samuele," I said, fidgeting with a cocktail napkin.

Samuele adjusted his glasses and quirked a smile. "*Ciao*, Trina." He paused and looked at Claudia. "And to you as well, Signorina…"

"Claudia," she finished. "Claudia Trevisani. Stefano's wife."

He blinked several times. "Ah! Now I remember you from the benefit concert a few days ago. I had no idea you and Stefano were…" He paused and looked around the crowd. "Is he here?"

Claudia chuckled. "Nah, it's just me and Trina tonight. Good show, by the way."

He returned his attention to Claudia and nodded. "*Grazie.* Thanks for coming. It is a pleasure to meet you, Claudia." He smiled at me. "And I am very glad you came, too, Trina."

My cheeks got hotter. I swallowed a lump in my throat.

Silence hung between us for a beat, then he finally said, "Hey, want to join me outside for a bit?"

The lump in my throat felt bigger. But then I wondered if Claudia would be okay. I looked her way, and the eager expression and encouraging nod she gave me were the answer to my silent question.

"Okay," I said to Samuele.

He turned and left. I watched him disappear out of the nightclub's side door.

"What are you waiting for?" Claudia's voice snapped me back to the present.

I stared at her rigid face. She pursed her lips.

Shaking off my trance, I awkwardly stood up and grabbed my purse. "Oh, right. I'll be back."

"Take your time," Claudia said, sitting back in her chair and swirling her third glass of Moscato of the night. She turned her attention to the new band onstage.

Outside around the building, I found Stefano and his friends packing their cars and chatting. Marco, the first to spot me, leaned over to Samuele and said something to him, causing him to look up as well. A bright smile spread across Samuele's face, and he started toward me. Marco patted Samuele's back, and he and the rest of his bandmates continued packing the cars.

Samuele stood before me and adjusted his glasses. I tugged nervously at the strap of my purse.

He stood so close, I could feel his warmth. "It is good to see you again, Trina."

"I told you I wouldn't miss it for the world." I gave a nervous laugh.

He pulled my hand from the purse strap, slowly brought it to his lips, and kissed the top. "I am glad you did not. I am fond of a woman who is true to her word. It brings out her inner beauty with integrity."

My breath hitched. His kiss sent goosebumps all over my body. *Oh my…*

He lifted his gaze until it met mine. He let go of my hand, and for a moment, I just stared into his beautiful green eyes.

He suddenly broke the stare and cleared his throat. "Ah, so. I just wanted to say that... you are a very interesting woman, and I was wondering if you wanted to get lunch with me sometime, or... maybe you and I can do a little jam session over at Marco's store." He grinned at the latter option.

My heart pounded faster. *He asked me to lunch? And to jam with him?* Surely, my ears were deceiving me. I opened my mouth to reply, but I was so stunned, no sound came out.

"I apologize if that was a little forward of me, *bella*," he continued.

"N-No, not at all. It was just a little unexpected. I would love to do those things with you. It would be fun. And..." I swallowed a lump in my throat. "I think you're interesting, too." *And so fine!*

His smile grew. "*Grazie*. We will make it a date. How about next week sometime?"

I thought about my planned schedule for next week, already trying to figure out how I would fit him into the mix—because I certainly was going to do everything in my power to include Samuele in my schedule. It would have been easy to cancel some outings to make the date—but cancelling plans had bugged me ever since I'd become a planner nerd.

"Okay, that sounds good. Why don't you call me and we can hash it out later?" I gave him my phone number.

He punched the info into his own cell phone and stuffed it in a back pocket of his jeans. A nervous look crossed his face, as though he had more to say. He licked his lips, and my eyes zeroed in on them with eager anticipation.

"Trina… there is a… ball tomorrow evening. I know it is such short notice, but I was wondering if you would like to go with me."

I blinked. "A ball?" Claudia had offered to pull some strings in order to allow me to attend a ball, but I'd declined. I mentally kicked myself for it.

"Sì. My name was put on the register, and I am expected to bring a guest. I had been so busy with my music to look for someone to go with that I did not realize the day was practically here. So would you like to go with me?"

This is surreal. Samuele Trevisani inviting me to a ball…I could be Cinderella for a night! But everything just sounded too good to be true; my rational side sensed that something just wasn't right. He probably had tons of other fans he could ask. Why me? "We've barely known each other for a few days. I would be honest and say that it is a bit odd for you to ask. Isn't there anyone else you'd rather go with?"

He looked at me intently. "There are others I could ask, but I would prefer you accompany me. You intrigue me, and I would love to get to know you more."

I fought down a smile. He was to the point but sweet, nonetheless. Of course I wanted to go, but that meant cancelling more scheduled outings. At that point, I was ready to throw my planner out the window just to be able to spend more time with him. It was a dangerous notion, because prior to becoming a planner addict, I'd been the most unorganized woman anyone had ever met. It was scary to think that I might become that woman again. Because this intriguing man was making me do all sorts of outrageous things. "I've never been to a ball before. I don't even have a dress for the occasion. It may not be a good idea…"

"That is okay, *bella*. I think everyone would understand that you are only visiting. Besides, if all you need is a dress, then I can arrange that…" He paused a beat. "Think about it, at least?"

I nodded, though I wasn't about to be the most underdressed person at a Trevisani ball. And I certainly wasn't going to let him buy me a brand-new dress that I would wear for all of a few hours. *Maybe Claudia will be able to help me out.*

He smiled, seemingly satisfied with my silent answer. His gaze focused on something beyond me for a moment, then it returned to me. "I suppose I should leave you and your friend to enjoy the rest of the night. I look forward to your decision about tomorrow."

"Leaving so soon, Samuele?"

I spun at the sound of Claudia's voice behind me. I stared at my friend, wide-eyed. "H-How long have you been there?"

She smirked. "Long enough to know that it's time for me to go." The way she said that sounded like she had another agenda. "It's almost midnight. Big day tomorrow, with getting ready for the ball and all." She raised her eyebrows slightly at me as a hint.

"But," I started to say, then Claudia shook her head.

"We'll talk later, girl. Why don't you let Samuele take you back to the hotel?"

Oh, I see her game. Fighting down another smile, I said, "I'm sure he's too busy or tired to do that. I mean, he just finished playing an almost-three-hour gig."

"I am not too busy or tired, *bella*," he interjected with a grin. He stood close to me again, his warmth giving me goosebumps.

I looked over my shoulder at him, blushing. "Are... are you sure? I mean..."

"It would be an honor."

I bit my bottom lip and looked sideways at Claudia, who still hadn't taken that smirk off her face. "*Ciao,*" she said, with an innocent wave then walked back to the limo, where her chauffeur was waiting.

I watched her leave, feeling slightly vulnerable for a moment, but then Samuele's presence eased that nervousness.

He extended his hand. "Shall we?"

I shifted my gaze to his hand then slowly took it. It was soft and warm as I remembered. He led me to his car, which was parked along the side of the building, with a few others.

"Where are your friends?" I asked.

"They already left." He opened the passenger door for me.

I slid in and got comfortable, then he closed the door and hopped in on the driver's side.

"You sure you don't mind taking me back to the hotel?" I said, breaking the awkward silence once he'd shut the driver's door.

He pressed a button near the steering wheel, starting the car. Then he looked at me deeply. "Of course not. What kind of man would I be to not offer to take you back?"

I blushed at his rhetorical-sounding question.

He took my hand and kissed the top. His lips lingered there as he watched me. "I still hope you consider going to the ball with me, *bella.*"

Speechless, I sucked in a breath. He was really putting on the charms, and I was totally under his spell. He finally let go of my hand and put the car in gear, then we were off. Samuele played some soft jazz music from the radio to take away the silence that resonated between us during the first few minutes of the trip. I occasionally snuck looks in his direction as light from the passing streetlamps swept across his face.

"I would have never thought you were friends with Claudia Trevisani," he finally said.

The comment took me by surprise. "Why is that so hard to believe? We've been best friends for a long time." *And she married your cousin.*

"I see."

His short answer didn't sit well with me. I looked at him with a raised eyebrow. "I know, by the way."

He mirrored my expression while keeping his eyes on the road. "You know? About?"

"You being a Trevisani."

He frowned slightly. "Did Claudia tell you?"

"No, Stefano did."

"Stefano?"

"Yes, your cousin? So when were you going to tell me that you were a Bellacignan royal?"

He glanced at me then back to the road. "I did not think that mattered to you."

I blinked, dumbfounded by the question. "Well… sure it does. It means you're a highly important person!"

He frowned. "Do you really base one's importance on their title or status?"

I opened my mouth to respond but bit my tongue as I thought deeply on his question. *Oh my goodness, what am I thinking?* "I didn't mean it the way it sounded. But if you're some duke or king or something, I would like to pay my respects and such."

"I am not a king or duke. I am Samuele. I do not want you to treat me differently because of my lineage or status. I want you to be yourself and treat me as you have been. Because that is what I really like about you."

I sucked in a breath. Sweat beaded on the bottoms of my palms, and I tried to wipe them on the seat. *He likes me?* How was I supposed to respond to something like that? I liked him, too, but wasn't entirely sure about him. He seemed bent on keeping his secrets locked away. "Have people treated you differently because of who you are?"

"For the most part, no, but I have heard stories of others in my family who were not so fortunate. I did not want to fall into a relationship when one does not show their true feelings."

I stared out the window as I thought on his words and felt two inches tall. He was right. I needed to see him as Samuele and nothing more than that. Though it would be extremely hard to look past the fact that he was related to Stefano. "I'm sorry, Samuele."

His frown lifted. "It is okay, *bella*."

Before I knew it, we were back at the hotel in Fiore Luna. An attendant spotted us, rushed over to place the Trevisani sign in front of the car, and returned to his post. Samuele turned off the car, took my hand, and kissed it gently as he looked at me. "Well? Have you made your decision?"

Momentarily lost in a daze, I stared at his lips atop my hand. I would never get tired of him doing that. I licked my lips then whispered, "Yes, I'll go to the ball with you." I sighed. *So much for visiting the street fair in Cittàcigni tomorrow afternoon.*

Samuele beamed widely, his face lighting up like a kid's on Christmas Day. He kissed my hand again more excitedly. "Oh, I am so happy, Trina. Tomorrow is going to be so wonderful.

So wonderful…

He released my hand, got out of the car, and walked around to the passenger's side to let me out. He took my hand in his and walked me to the entrance. We stopped at the revolving doors, and I turned to him. "So, after tomorrow's ball, then what? Will we see each other again?"

Samuele chuckled. "*Ovviamente*, we both agreed on a date. And I still want to jam with you."

Yeah, I'm sure we can both make some beautiful music together. I chuckled to myself at the cheesy thought. "When's your next gig?"

One corner of his mouth turned upward into a crooked smile. "Tuesday evening. I will be playing at an outdoor charity event for my cousin's foundation in Alta Rosa."

"Stefano?" I raised my eyebrows.

"No, another cousin. Alessio."

Alessio. Is he a duke, too? Maybe a prince? I smiled, wishing it hadn't mattered so much, but I couldn't help myself. It wasn't often I was around the company of royals. But still, I needed to remind myself of Samuele's request. "That's great. Do you think I can come watch you play again?"

His smile returned. "You can come watch me play anytime. But do you know what would be really great?"

"Hmm?"

"Playing in a band together. You and I. Jamming it out."

I gasped at the unexpected notion. "You know that can never happen. I'm only in Bellacigna for another week, then I'm headed back to South Carolina."

He shrugged. "It was just a thought. Marco is thinking about leaving the band so that he can concentrate more on running his music store, so we would be without a bassist. And I do not know about you, but jazz without bass is just not jazz."

"I'm sure you'll find a replacement soon enough," I said.

"Perhaps." He paused and looked to the revolving door. "Well, then. You have a good night, *bella*." He took both of my hands and rubbed them gently. Then he brought them both to his lips and kissed them. I shivered in delight.

"Good… goodnight," I said breathlessly.

He tilted his head then returned to his car. I continued staring as he drove off until his taillights were no longer in sight.

CHAPTER 5

SATURDAY MORNING, THE OBNOXIOUS RINGING of the hotel phone next to the bed woke me. Groaning, I rolled over in bed and blindly groped for the receiver.

"*Buongiorno*, Signorina Mauer," Erudito's warm voice greeted from the phone. "I hope I did not wake you."

I sat up in bed. "Oh, no. I was, ah… just reading," I said, trying to make my voice sound alert.

"Ah, *bene*. I am calling to inform you that Signora Stacson wishes to meet with you as soon as possible."

I blinked, wide awake now. "Why? Is everything okay?"

"Sì, everything is fine. There is just a certain matter that she wishes to discuss."

His cryptic message wasn't very comforting, but the thought of being able to see my literary idol again outweighed my suspicions. "Uh… okay… I'll get ready as soon as I can."

"*Ottimo.* I am on my way to the hotel now. I will be waiting for you in the lobby."

I hopped in the shower and got dressed and ready in record time. I took the elevator down to the lobby and discovered Erudito casually chatting with one of the female attendants. The attendant spotted me first and pointed. Erudito followed her gaze and smiled.

He tipped his black hat as I approached. "Ready to go?"

I returned the smile. "As ready as I'll ever be."

He escorted me to a limo parked outside and opened the back door for me. I climbed in and got settled, then he took the wheel. The drive was silent as I stared out the window at the passing city. My mind was racing, and finally, I couldn't take any more of the endless silence. "So what does she want to talk to me about?"

"I do not know, Signorina. I was not privy to that information. But I trust it is good news."

A thousand and one ideas popped into my head. *Will she let me get a sneak peek of her newest book?* My heart pounded. What I wouldn't give to be a part of her next bestseller.

We pulled up in front of Adelina's mansion, and Erudito let me out. He led me to the front door and handed me off to the maid waiting there. Though the maid was not the one I'd met before, she seemed just as sweet in her mannerisms. She escorted me to the courtyard, where Adelina sat in her usual spot at the tiny table for two, sipping coffee. Her head was tilted, and her gaze was focused on a notepad in her lap. The maid cleared her throat, and Adelina looked up with a start. Her face softened when she recognized us.

"*Buongiorno,* Trina! So wonderful to see you." Adelina gestured to the empty seat across from her. "Please sit."

I hesitated then looked back at the maid, but she had already returned to the house. Facing Adelina once more, with slight trepidation, I slowly lowered myself onto the empty chair. "Thank you for inviting me again."

She poured me a cup of the strong-smelling coffee and slid it over to me. "When my brother told me the news, I knew this was the right thing to do. I was hoping that you would come."

"I would never miss out on an opportunity to see my favorite author." I lifted my cup, then realization hit me. I set the cup back down. "Wait… you have a brother?"

With a slightly guilty look on her face, she averted her eyes and traced her finger around the rim of her cup. "Sì. His name is Samuele."

I blinked in disbelief. "Samuele Trevisani is your brother?"

"Sì, can you not tell?" She looked back at me again, and it was then I recognized those same signature green eyes that Samuele had. Yes, there was no mistaking that she was related to him.

"I had no idea…" was all I could say.

"Forgive me, but I had no idea that you knew my brother. Honestly, I have not talked to him in weeks, because he was always busy with his music career. But I was so surprised when he contacted me very late last night and told me all about you and your willingness to go with him to this evening's ball. He was unable to attend last year because he was in London. He was hesitant in attending this year because there would be a lot of couples attending. But last night, he could not stop talking about you."

I swallowed. It seemed like such a farfetched notion that they could be related, even though they had similar looks. It couldn't be true, could it?

"You have no idea how happy I am for him, Trina," Adelina continued. "His last relationship ended months ago, and that was short-lived and better left unsaid. I am so happy for him now."

"Whoa," I stopped her, holding up my hands. "We're not dating or anything. We're just going to the ball. That's a huge difference."

She smiled coyly at me. "If I did not know any better, I would say that you are quite fond of my brother, by the way your face lit up at his mention."

Am I really that obvious? "He's okay. Sweet and quite talented on the drums. But we're not in a serious relationship or anything." I rested the brim of my coffee cup against my lips, not knowing why I'd felt a twinge of guilt when I said that.

But Adelina seemed satisfied with my reply and took another sip of her coffee. "Regardless, I am glad to know that you are going with him, and I would like to offer you a gift, which was my main reason for summoning you here." She got up from her chair and extended her hand. "Come."

Curious, I stood and gently took her hand. She led me out of the courtyard and through a set of cherrywood doors that opened to a grand master bedroom that looked three times bigger than my entire studio apartment. Morning light filtered through the matching cherrywood-finished floor-to-ceiling windows, accented with giant blue velvety curtains. Golden beams touched marble columns, statues, and pottery on display, and other expensive-looking decorations dotted the room. A small fountain set against one of the walls gave off a steady, relaxing trickling sound. I stared for several moments at the giant, unfathomable bed that looked as big as three king-sized beds put together. It must've taken hours just to make up the bed every morning, and climbing into it was probably a chore, too.

Adelina opened another set of doors, revealing a massive walk-in closet that looked more like a high-end department store. Clothes of all styles and colors hung from racks or were folded neatly on the gold shelves of one wall. Endless pairs of shoes lined the other three walls. My mother, who was a shoe fanatic, would have died if she'd seen it. The sight took my breath away—and it was only the closet!

We snaked through the sea of racks and came across a single wooden door, which led to another, smaller closet area that contained formal gowns in various styles and colors.

I widened my eyes. *I've literally stepped into heaven.* "This is truly amazing," I said.

"*Grazie.* I am a bit of a… shopper, if you have not already guessed." She chuckled and gestured to the gowns. "Take your pick."

My jaw dropped. "Wait. What? Are you serious?"

"Sì. You and I seem to be of similar height and size. With a few minor adjustments, the dress you choose will be a perfect fit, I am certain."

"I… I can't possibly…"

"I insist, Trina. You need a dress for the ball, and I have more dresses than I know what to do with. Besides, there is no one I would want to do this for more than an avid fan like you who appreciates my hard work."

My eyes burned. I was definitely going to break down right there if she kept that up. I couldn't pull myself together fast enough. Though I didn't think myself worthy of such a fabulous gift, Adelina's overly kind gesture seemed so sincere and genuine, just like in the stories that she wrote. No wonder I loved her so much.

Finally giving in to her insistence, I took a deep breath and perused the gowns for several long minutes, taking in all of their beautiful styles and colors. I finally settled on a vibrant purple off-the-shoulder gown with silver trim. As I reached out to touch it, Adelina gasped, and I quickly withdrew my hand.

"Oh! *Ottima scelta*, Trina! This was one of my favorite dresses."

My shoulders slumped. Just my luck I would choose the one dress that was her favorite. No way she would want to give that to me. *But how cool is it that we have the same tastes in clothing?* "Oh, sorry. I'll choose another one."

"No! I want you to wear this dress. I think you will represent it well."

My cheeks flushed. "Wow, Adelina. Is this really for real? I mean… here I am, with you in this magical place, and you offer me one of your cherished gowns. I just can't believe—"

She laughed. "You have come a long way, and I want your stay here in my country to be a memorable one. And besides, you're going to the ball with my brother! I must make sure you look…" She licked her lips. "Like a princess."

"Honestly, I don't see anything happening between us after tonight." *Though I certainly wouldn't mind.* "I'm not good with long-distance relationships, y'know? But I'll always love the fact that he's so passionate about his music."

Adelina took the purple dress from the rack and held it up to me, studying the size and shape against my figure. It looked like it would fit as is, but Adelina seemed to have a good eye for that sort of thing. "Sì, music is his passion," she replied absently. "Our parents thought it was an odd hobby for him to pick up at the time, all things considering. I mean, he has quite a future ahead of him, and he somehow manages to balance his life and his music really well. I do admire him a lot."

I wrinkled my brow. "Why admire him? You're a bestselling author."

"Sì, but time is so precious, especially when you are writing. And there are not enough hours in a day when you are trying to keep up with your daily life. Samuele, on the other hand, seems to have mastered that part down.

"Writing is not always as simple as you think. Sometimes I get mindblocks, which prevent me from writing, so I go out and visit a nearby town, help out around the community, and other things to help relax and clear my mind to be able to write again." She headed toward the closet exit. "I will call my tailor, who will do some minor alterations."

I followed her out, passing a clock, which read 1:05. Only six more hours until the ball. My heart pounded nervously in anticipation of seeing Samuele all dressed up. I needed to head back to the hotel to shower and get my hair in order. Just my hair alone would take a few hours to get manageable again. Adelina informed me that the gown would be delivered to my suite once her tailor finished with the alterations. I couldn't wait another second.

I'd agreed to go to the ball with Samuele, and Adelina had sealed the deal by offering me one of her favorite gowns. *No backing out now.*

That afternoon, while I was in the bathroom working on my hair, my cell phone rang from the master bedroom. I wanted to ignore the call, but then I realized it could be Adelina letting me know the dress had arrived. Or Claudia. Or…

I scrambled out of the bathroom and snatched my cell from the desk. "Hello?"

"*Ciao*, Trina."

My whole body melted at the sound of Samuele's voice. "Hi, Samuele."

"I hope I am not disturbing you."

"Oh, not at all, just getting ready for tonight."

"Ah, *bene.*"

"Adelina is letting me borrow one of her beautiful gowns for the occasion. Why didn't you tell me you two were related?"

"I had no idea you knew my sister."

"Your sister is my most favorite romance author ever."

He laughed. "Sì, she seems to be a lot of people's favorite. I am proud of what she is doing. And I am glad that she was able to help you get a dress."

"You didn't have to do all this, you know. Neither of you did."

"I know, but I wanted to. I am just glad that you agreed to go to the ball with me. I am very excited."

"Me, too."

"The ball starts at seven tonight. I will pick you up around six thirty, okay?"

I checked the clock. I had an hour left to finish getting ready. "Sounds good."

We said our goodbyes and hung up. My hotel phone rang shortly after. It was the front desk letting me know my gown had arrived. The timing couldn't have been any sweeter. The day was getting overwhelmingly amazing. After hanging up with the front desk, I hugged myself, grinning like a fool. *Eat your heart out, Cinderella.*

Chapter 6

I CHECKED MYSELF IN THE FULL-LENGTH MIRROR for what had to have been the hundredth time. I truly felt like I was living Cinderella's life. I just hoped this fairy-tale fantasy would last beyond midnight.

After yet another check of the gown and two more extra checks of my hair, which I'd spent a good two hours getting situated, I headed down to the lobby. I garnered admiring glances from some of the other guests as I passed. My tall, dark, and overwhelmingly handsome Prince Charming was waiting in the lobby, with his hands in his tuxedo pockets, while he talked with some of the awe-struck female guests. Samuele, his hair slicked back, looked my way and beamed. He brushed past the guests and made his way toward me. Taking my hands in his, he scanned me up and down from head to toe then settled his emerald gaze on my face.

"You look *bellisima*, Trina," he said breathlessly.

Feeling my cheeks get hot, I tried to fight down a smile. "Thank you. So do you."

My arm in his, he escorted me to the exit. The guests and hotel staff continued watching us as if we were a celebrity couple. And somewhere in my fantasies, I thought we were. Sitting outside the hotel in the Trevisani-designated parking spot was a black stretch limousine. The back door was open, and a tall, stoic chauffeur stood outside. He nodded to the two of us as we approached. Samuele helped me into the backseat then climbed in after me. The chauffeur shut the door, took the wheel, and set off.

Samuele flipped a hidden switch on the back of the passenger's seat, and a tinted partition rose, separating us from the driver. It suddenly became a little quieter, too. Samuele sat back in his seat and looked over at me. "Are you comfortable?"

"Yes, thank you." Smiling, I scooted closer to him.

He rested his hand on mine. "I am so glad you decided to come with me. Tonight is going to be great."

I looked at our hands, and my heart began to pound furiously.

"You know," he continued, "it has only been five days, but I feel as though I have known you for far longer."

I sucked in a breath.

"You make me laugh and smile. And you are unlike other girls I have met."

"Why? Because I play the bass?" I laughed.

He paused then laughed, too. "It is not just that. You have a certain charm about you. Personality. You are fun to talk to." He looked at me deeply. "I like that."

I swallowed a lump forming in my throat. *What is he trying to say?* I'd never had a guy tell me such sweet, romantic things like that. "T-Thank you," was all I could muster.

He chuckled at my obvious fluster. "Hey, let us do a little jam session at Marco's store tomorrow, if you are up to it, that is."

"I'm always up for a jam session. It's a date."

"*Infatti.*" He opened a secret compartment in the back of the seat, revealing a cooler with a wine bottle within. He retrieved two glasses from beside the compartment and filled them both with the sparkling liquid. He handed me a glass.

I took it graciously, gave a little sniff, then took a sip. My eyes went wide. I'd never tasted wine so amazing. It was blended perfectly with just the right sweetness.

His brow wrinkled. "Do you not like it?"

"What? No! I *love* it! This is the best wine I've ever tasted. Where did you get it? I need to pick up a few cases of this to take home."

The troubled look on his face disappeared, and he smiled. "It is from my family's vineyard. It is only sold in a few select premium shops around Bellacigna."

My shoulders slumped. "In other words, this wine costs more than my entire life savings."

He chuckled. "I can give you a few bottles, if you so desire."

"What! No, don't do that. Your family is running a business. Don't steal the inventory."

"It is not stealing, *bella*. The inventory is just as much mine as it is the rest of my family's."

I shook my head insistently. "No, please, forget I ever mentioned anything about this awesome wine." I inhaled every last drop from my glass.

Samuele offered to pour me another, but I reluctantly refused. No doubt, there was probably more like it at the ball.

"So, are you going to be playing drums at the ball, too?" I asked.

"No, I am just attending, like the rest of the guests. An orchestra has been hired for the event."

"Wow."

"Sì, the Alta Rosa Symphony Orchestra. One of the most prestigious in all of Europe. Formal gatherings like these are always a big deal for my family. All of the proceeds from the event go toward the Trevisani Foundation for Purity. It is our largest foundation that helps millions of undeserved children and families around the world each year have access to clean drinking water."

My heart swelled. If there was one thing I loved, that was a philanthropist. And much of the Trevisani family seemed very passionate about their generosity and determination to help others in need.

Thirty minutes later, we arrived in Alta Rosa, Bellacigna's capital. The city was lit up like Las Vegas with so many clubs, restaurants, and small shops flourishing with business. Alta Rosa was the last place on my list of spots to visit before my vacation ended. I plastered my face against the window of the limo, staring at the passing lights and people walking to and fro, many dressed as though they were about to live up the night.

"This is amazing…" I said breathily.

Samuele leaned over to me, his cheek close to mine as he drew his face close to the same window. The heat of his body so close to mine gave me chills. "Alta Rosa is a beautiful city. I enjoy coming here when I have gigs."

I turned my head slightly, staring at Samuele in my peripheral vision. His outdoorsy cedar scent tickled my senses. Samuele leaned back into his seat, taking with it his inviting warmth.

We reached the heart of the city, and the limo parked along the curb in front of the venue, a massive, old-style palace crafted from white marble. The wide shallow steps leading up to the main entrance were lit with tea candles, creating a path of glimmering white. Marble statues of regal-looking men and women in ancient garb were posted in shallow alcoves on the building's second story. Two statues of tallstanding lions flanked the main entrance.

The chauffeur opened the limo's door, and we got out. The air was cool and fresh as we walked arm in arm up the stairs among the sea of people dressed in suits, tuxedos, and colorful gowns. Several guests glanced our way, and a few even approached Samuele, saying something to him in Italian and giving him respectful bows and curtseys.

Of course Samuele's important. He's a Trevisani, I reminded myself. Though I wasn't sure where he sat in his family's hierarchy, just being in the family must've had its perks.

Entering the palace's interior grand hall, I was reminded of the awe-inspiring beauty of the Verde Suites hotel in Fiore Luna. The old-style, mahogany-and-marble architecture and giant floor-to-ceiling windows had a certain rustic charm that fit well with the formal atmosphere. We passed under crystal chandeliers hanging from the open ceiling. They created tiny white-and-rainbow-colored moving dots along the polished mahogany floor. My ears were drawn to light, cheery orchestral music coming from a corner of the grand hall, where a band of fifteen formally dressed men and women played violins, cellos, and flutes.

Many people, young and old, dressed in all of their finest glam and glitter, were gathered on the main floor, as well as the upper floor and balconies, which were decorated with silver garland and white Christmas lights.

I could practically feel the royalty—if the majority of the guests really were of the Trevisani family. Or perhaps they were just very, very rich.

Samuele squeezed my hand gently, and I snapped out of my thoughts. Smiling, he gestured toward a giant spiral staircase at the end of the hall, leading up to the second floor. I eagerly followed his lead. The crowds parted, creating a path for us as we walked, some staring at us in admiration. All of them paid Samuele their respects with bows and curtseys. With a plastered-on smile, Samuele gave them a light wave.

"Why so modest?" I muttered to him as we climbed the stairs. "It must be nice being a Trevisani noble. I bet even the family dog gets this same kind of attention."

He looked at me and frowned. "I would prefer my respect is earned through my own skill and hard work, not luck."

I raised an eyebrow. "Luck? What do you mean?"

Before he could answer, a familiar face nearly knocked me to the ground with a giant hug. Startled, my body tensed but quickly relaxed at the sight of my best friend.

"You made it, Trina!" Claudia exclaimed, squeezing me tighter.

I grunted. "Ugh. You, too…" I said, out of breath.

She finally let go—thank goodness—and we admired each other's gowns. Claudia's glamorous and baby-blue dress flowed around her body like a waterfall. Her silver shoes, which sparkled as much as the chandeliers, matched the silver-trimmed Grecian neckline. The only jewelry she wore were a pair of silver earrings, a black choker with a tiny blue sapphire amulet, and a silver tiara in her thick, curly hair.

"You look like a real duchess—no, a princess," I said.

Claudia beamed. "So do you, girl! Didn't think you'd attend a royal ball on your vacation, huh?"

I laughed. "Never." I looked over at Samuele, who had gone off to chat with other guests. He occasionally glanced my way, offering a small smile before turning back to his conversation. I noticed many of the guests had a familiar air about them, from the way they walked to their general mannerisms. I spotted Adelina among the crowd, and her escort—Erudito! The two of them made such a cute couple. I also noticed Stefano walking about, a glass of wine in hand, making light conversation. He stopped at a cluster of people gathered on the opposite side of the hall.

"There are so many people everywhere…" I whispered.

"Yeah, this annual event is a big deal for the Trevisani family. They receive so many sponsors and donations for their foundation."

I nodded. "It's good to know that all this glitz and glamor is for a good cause." I looked around. "So why aren't we downstairs, dancing with the other guests?"

Claudia laughed. "There'll be plenty of time for that. Your feet are going to be aching before the night is over." She paused, glancing over the balcony, and her face brightened. "Oh! Come with me. I need to introduce you." She grabbed my hand and pulled me toward the stairs.

I hurried as fast as my shoes would let me, stepping ever so carefully so that I didn't trip on my dress. Downstairs, Claudia tugged me through the crowd of guests mingling and dancing, and finally, we stopped at a woman who had her back turned, standing next to a man in a motorized wheelchair.

Claudia inclined her head to the couple. "*Mi scusi, Vostre Altezze Reali,*" she said in slow, awkward Italian that was tinged with a hint of her Southern accent.

The couple turned. My jaw dropped. My gaze immediately fixed on the woman, who looked heavenly in her beautiful white gown. A diamond tiara was tucked neatly in her up-do. Her icy-blue eyes traveled from Claudia to me, and her soft, powdered face glowed as she greeted us with a heartwarming smile. The man in the wheelchair studied us briefly then smiled, as well.

I gasped, following Claudia's lead, and bowed my head to King Gaspare and Queen Elisa, the king and queen of Bellacigna. I clasped my hands together to contain my excitement. "Y-Your Royal Highnesses!" I stammered. "It is such an honor!"

"May I introduce my best friend from America, Trina Mauer," Claudia said to the couple as she gestured to me.

I swear, I will never forget this day in my life when I met the king and queen.

The night went on, and I met more of the Trevisani family. Claudia was right—their family was huge! Talking to them was like talking to everyday people instead of royals. They were so down to earth and loved to have fun.

Later, Samuele and I finally danced with the rest of the family and guests. I had two left feet when it came to waltzing, but Samuele was so patient with me. We often danced close, and his warmth was inviting. During one song, Claudia and I danced together. We laughed and spun around like young fairy-tale princesses. After dancing through five lengthy songs, my feet were on fire. Samuele helped me up the stairs to sit with the family. I plopped down with a sigh on a plush chaise near the balcony. Samuele sat next to me.

"That was fun, *bella*," he said, rubbing my bare back.

I shivered beneath his warm touch and smiled. "Yeah, it was. I've never done ballroom dancing before."

"You are a natural."

The music faded, and I peered over the edge of the balcony at the king and queen, who were in the middle of the hall, with guests gathered around them. King Gaspare's regal voice came through loud and clear over the grand hall's hidden sound system, garnering all of the attendees' attention. He spoke first in Italian then again in English as he explained the purpose of this event and the number of sponsors and donors who had contributed.

Samuele leaned over to me and said in a low tone, "Almost everyone in my family has a charity or foundation. Many times, someone will donate to their charity, as well as the Trevisani Foundation for Purity, which is the family's main foundation. When that happens, then the family matches that donation."

I nodded. "Do you have a foundation or charity, too?"

"Sì, mine is called the Calandra Music Scholarship Fund. Established in honor of my late grandmother, Calandra Russo, who was an amazing singer. The scholarship provides assistance to thousands of less-fortunate high school students who want to study music in college."

"That's great. You know, Stefano recently started that new art and music program at the university in Cittàcigni."

He nodded. "The foundation awarded one hundred and fifty students last year."

King Gaspare continued reading down the list—in Italian and English—and the audience clapped when appropriate. Each of the Trevisani members waved to the applauding crowd as they were addressed.

"Next is the Food for Global Health charity, headed by His Grace Duke Stefano Trevisani of Cittàcigni."

My attention piqued at the mention of Stefano's name.

"Last year," the king continued, "the charity received forty-six thousand, nine-hundred and eighty-nine euros in donations. One hundred and twenty donors gave nineteen thousand, two hundred euros, which Duke Stefano will match. Thank you for your generosity."

Stefano walked out to King Gaspare and spun, waving to everyone. Claudia stood by, clapping wildly, as well. Stefano gave a hug and kiss to the king and queen then disappeared back into the crowd, along with Claudia.

I felt Samuele's hand over mine, and he gave it a small squeeze. I looked over at him, and he gestured toward the king with a small tilt of his head. *Was he about to get called next?*

"And next is the Calandra Music Scholarship Fund, headed by His Royal Highness, Prince Samuele Trevisani."

Prince. I blinked as realization suddenly set in. *Prince!*

The king's voice was a blur of noise in my ears. Samuele wasn't a duke or a regular noble who just happened to hold the Trevisani title. He was a real-life, honest-to-goodness *prince*! I pulled my hand out from under his. I opened my mouth to speak, but the audience suddenly erupted in applause, and Samuele stood from the chaise and waved to the crowd from the balcony. He gently tugged my arm, urging me to stand with him. But I felt as though the wind had been knocked out of me. I remained planted on the chaise.

Samuele looked down at me and frowned. He waited for the audience to settle again, and while the king continued, he asked, "Why are you so upset?"

I looked at him with a mix of emotions. Was I upset? I didn't want to be. I'd discovered my handsome Prince Charming—everything was perfect. But unfortunately, the dream wouldn't last long since I would be leaving it all behind in a few days, once the vacation was over. "I… I'm not upset," I finally replied. I met Claudia's gaze from below. She had that look in her eye that said, "Meeting in the ladies' room. Now." I looked back at Samuele. "I need to use the restroom. Will you excuse me a moment?"

"*Certo.*" He helped me down the stairs and allowed me to walk on my own to the restroom.

Claudia soon followed in my footsteps, and I could sense her wheels were turning.

As soon as the door to the ladies' room closed, I checked under every stall door to ensure we were alone. Afterward, I looked to Claudia, wide-eyed. "Did you know?"

Claudia shook her head. "I really had no idea. Not everyone of the family are in succession to the throne. And it doesn't help that many tend to be incognito about their status for whatever reason."

"He thought I would treat him differently if I'd known," I said, more to myself than to Claudia.

Claudia's eyebrow rose. "Really? Well it would make sense, I guess. Stefano sorta did that to me, too."

"I can't believe it. He's a real-life prince. And he *likes* me." I frowned.

She cocked her head to the side. "So why that look?"

"Because I will never see him again, come Wednesday when I head back to the States." Once my vacation was over, it was back to my normal routine life at Lala Latte. Anything that happened here in Bellacigna would be only a memory.

She mirrored my frown. "I'm sure he can come visit you sometime."

I shrugged. "Maybe, but long-distance relationships never work. It's just my luck that the man of my dreams has to live thousands of miles across the ocean." It was my fault for getting attached to him, even though a part of me had known it would be a bad idea. Claudia had told me all about how busy Stefano had gotten once he'd begun his official duties as duke. Between that and his occasional deejaying gigs, Claudia barely saw him on some days, but it didn't seem to bother her much. I knew that wouldn't be easy for me if Samuele got too busy with life.

"It's almost midnight. At least enjoy the rest of the ball with him and forget about all this for just a minute."

Almost midnight. Once the clock struck twelve, the fantasy would disappear. "I'll try."

Claudia and I left the ladies' room. Most of the family and guests were out on the floor, dancing to the lively orchestral music. Samuele was standing at the bottom of the stairs, watching them, until his eyes cut to me and Claudia. Smiling, he swept over to us.

"May I have this last dance, *bella*?" he said, taking my hand.

I caught Claudia's pointed look as she walked past us and went to find Stefano. I turned back to Samuele and forced a smile. "Okay."

He led me to the floor with the other dancers, and I followed his graceful lead into a slow waltz. I felt his hand touch the bare skin of my back. We gazed at each other as the world around us spun. I inhaled his scent, adoring his warmth. I didn't want him to let me go. My body was betraying my mind.

He spun me around then drew me into him.

"Why didn't you tell me you were a prince?" I whispered once we were close.

Not faltering in his steps, he spun me back around then rested his hand at the small of my back. He dipped me back ever so slightly, and his face hovered close to mine. My eyes drew down to his lips, anticipating them touching mine.

"Does my status truly matter to you?" He straightened me, and I fell in step with him again.

I frowned, disappointed by the completely valid question, and the fact that he hadn't kissed me. "No, I was just curious. Does this mean you'll be the next king of Bellacigna?"

"No, I am twenty-fourth in line to the throne." He spun me in his arms then unwound me like a top.

"So if you are a prince, does that mean your sister Adelina is a—"

"Princess, sì. But she prefers to keep her status a secret as she concentrates on her books."

"I see." I glanced at the crowd and spotted Adelina and Erudito dancing together.

Samuele followed my gaze. "*Oh, che bello.* I *thought* there might be something going on between those two."

We finished the last dance, and midnight struck. After saying goodbye to the family, friends, and guests, Samuele and I followed the crowd to the exit and into the waiting limo. It was pretty silent throughout the trip, though both of us were exhausted after a long night. But the silence did nothing to calm my nerves as my mind continuously raced over my conversation with Claudia.

We pulled up to the hotel, and the chauffeur opened the door for me. As I scooted to slide out of the backseat, Samuele placed his hand over mine. I paused and looked over at him.

"I had a good time tonight, Trina. *Grazie.*"

I smiled. "It was fun. Thank you for this memorable night."

"Meet me at *Dolce Sinfonia* tomorrow at two o'clock, okay?"

I blinked. I'd nearly forgotten about our "date." I hadn't forgotten a *single* important date since I'd found planner peace. But I'd also never had a man put such a crazy spell on me, either. "Sounds good. I'll see you then."

His smile grew, then he slowly leaned over and planted a kiss on my lips. Time had stopped. My body froze under the gentle touch of his lips on mine, and his sweet, invigorating taste of a royal dessert. The moment was over before it began, and he pulled back and let my hand go. "*Buonanotte*, Trina."

My head swam from the rush of emotions that shot through my brain. I got out of the limo awkwardly with the help of the chauffeur, steadied myself, then left the beautiful fantasy behind me as I stepped through the revolving doors of the hotel.

CHAPTER 7

I COULD BARELY SLEEP, DESPITE ARRIVING AT MY suite at almost one in the morning—I couldn't stop replaying that goodnight kiss Samuele had given me in the limo. Though it had thrown me for a loop, it was a more-than-perfect way to end a night. I was up way too early for my own good on Monday and couldn't get back to sleep. I had made plans to go sightseeing around Alta Rosa later in the morning, and as much as I wanted to see more of the country, I was more excited to jam out with Samuele. The man had totally put a monkey wrench in my planning routine. And part of me kind of liked it.

It was only seven thirty in the morning, and I decided to do the unthinkable and cancel my sightseeing trip to Royal Rose Lake just north of the city in favor of remaining in Fiore Luna and near the music store. I must've been seriously anxious and lovestruck over the date if I felt the urge to cancel my plans. But I'd promised myself I would get back on track as soon as I returned home and all the handsome royal distractions were gone. I ate a small breakfast and walked around the city. By one o'clock—almost an hour before the date—I made my way to the music store. It wasn't just the anxiety; I also couldn't resist the urge to play around on those awesome basses again. Marco might want to challenge me to another play-off.

The bells jingled as I entered the store. Some customers walked about, while a few tested out the keyboards in one section, but there was no sign of Samuele. Marco was alone at the register, deep in a conversation on the phone. His back turned, he didn't seem to notice me.

"*Cosa devo fare?*" Marco said. "*Concerto di domani potrebbe essere una potenziale grande opportunità per noi.*" He balled his hand into a fist and shook it as he spoke in angry Italian. "*Non posso credere che non avrebbe ottenuto malato in un momento come questo!*"

He paused, then his shoulders slumped, and he sighed. *"Va bene... Ci vediamo quando si arriva qui. Ciao."*

Leaving him to his conversation, I headed straight for the basses in the back and picked out a different one to play. I finally felt bold enough to choose the black-and-purple fretless. *Marco* did *say that I could try out any of them in the store, so...*

The instrument didn't feel all that different from the fretted basses that I was used to playing, but it was intriguing to try nonetheless. I found a spot to sit and plugged the bass into an amplifier. I plucked some strings, familiarizing myself with where all the notes were. It was definitely less forgiving than my fretted bass when it came to finger positioning exactly on the spot. I imagined Daisy Weatherspoon on stage, playing one of her up-and-down jazz riffs that she was famous for. I attempted something similar but failed miserably four notes in.

"Welcome back, Signorina Trina."

I started at the closeness of Marco's voice. I looked up from the instrument. He watched me with amusement in his eyes.

"Hi, Marco," I said, blushing. I lowered my head, trying to focus on my finger positioning again, but it was hard to concentrate, knowing Marco was watching my every move. I tried tuning out the world around me by strumming some chords until one sounded vaguely familiar. It was a song I'd heard Samuele's band play a couple nights ago. I somehow remembered every note. I guess it was due to my being enthralled by Samuele's drum solo in the beginning. My eyes closed, I began playing, envisioning being on stage with Samuele as he played his drums, and I could hear his perfect rhythm. I played the main bass parts of the entire song, then again with the lead guitar parts. I became lost in my own fantasy: Samuele and I playing together on stage and traveling the world. *Me and my real-life Prince Charming as worldwide jazz superstars.*

I ended my song with a final strum and wiggled my finger on the last note to give it that "mwah" sound until it faded out completely. I opened my eyes, awakening from the musical trance. I suddenly heard a few people in the store clapping. When my mind finally returned to the present, I realized that my little mini-concert had garnered an audience. Some of the customers had gathered around, gawking. Marco clapped enthusiastically, beaming.

"*Eccellente!*" Marco exclaimed.

The audience stopped clapping, except for one person who continued to clap, slow and steady. Everyone turned to the man—Samuele—who stood nearby, wearing a dark-green button-down shirt with the sleeves rolled up his arms. His emerald-green eyes stared deep into mine, and I swallowed. *Oh my goodness. How long was he there watching me play?*

I chewed my bottom lip then gave a timid bow of my head. "T-Thank you," I said, more to the crowd.

Samuele finally stopped clapping and approached me. The rest of the audience broke away and resumed their browsing around the store, and Marco left to tend to the customers.

"I recognized that song," Samuele said. "*Il Mockingbird.* We played it at Heaven and Blues."

I blinked. "Oh, I didn't know the title. I was just playing it by ear."

"That was amazing that you can even do that. And you play the lead and bass parts so well. I am impressed."

All his flattery was spoiling me way too much… not that I was complaining or anything. "Thanks, but I'm nowhere near as good as you and your bandmates."

He raised his eyebrows. "I highly doubt that." He nodded toward another part of the store, where the drums were. "Let us jam a bit."

Grinning, I unplugged the bass and followed him with it. I found another spot to set up again, and Samuele situated himself behind an electric padded drum set on display. He turned it on and tested it by striking all the pads in various patterns and sequences.

"Wow, you can actually play that thing?" I asked, amazed by the odd setup.

He laughed. "It is a far cry from the traditional drums I am used to playing, but it still does the job."

We played several songs, a few from Samuele's band, including *"Il Mockingbird."* Our sounds complemented each other. Whenever I played more demandingly, he struck the drums more forcefully. When I backed off, he played more subtly. Playing with him felt so easy, so natural, as if I'd always been a part of his band.

It was almost closing time for the shop when we were forced to end our lengthy jam session. We'd ended up playing for three hours, with few breaks in between, and we'd talked about our favorite music artists and our most embarrassing moments of playing in a band. Marco certainly didn't mind us jamming out for so long, as it attracted many customers in his store. But like all good things, the session finally came to an end, and Samuele walked me back to the hotel.

"While I enjoyed the ball last night, hanging out with you today was even better," he said, then looked over to me. "You are truly a gifted musician, Trina."

I beamed. "Thanks, but you're the real gift to music. Playing with another musician never felt so easy before now. Even my own bandmates from college weren't always so quick to adapt to certain songs the way you are."

Fighting down a smile, he shoved his hands in his pockets. "*Grazie.* You are too kind."

We arrived at the hotel and stood at the foot of the shallow stairs that led up to the entrance. Samuele withdrew his hands from his pockets and took my hands. He stared deep into my eyes. "Trina, there is something I wish to ask of you."

I gulped. *That look.* I'd seen it before, during a past relationship that had gone sour. Desire. It was no secret that Samuele and I were fond of each other, and this "talk" was bound to happen sooner or later. I just wasn't ready for it yet. How far would our relationship go? In two days, I would be on a plane back to America, and I would never see Samuele again. Claudia thought Samuele could easily come visit me whenever he wanted, but I knew he wouldn't, with all the gigs he did almost every night. Once I was gone, he would move on from me. Long-distance relationships never worked.

My throat tightened. Butterflies filled my stomach at the thought of what he intended to ask, because I didn't know how I was going to answer. I liked Samuele more than I should have, and I would probably never get over him once I left Bellacigna.

I closed my eyes and took a long, deep breath. I opened my eyes. "Yes? What is it?"

He pursed his lips and looked thoughtful about something. "I have been informed that our keyboardist, Castello, has fallen ill and is unable to play at our gig tomorrow night. Thankfully, he had taught enough for Marco to be able to fill in for him during times like these. However, that means we are without a bassist..." He let the statement hang as he gave me a pleading look.

My brain didn't fully comprehend at the moment what he was trying to say, so I looked at him with raised eyebrows, waiting for him to go on.

"This is a very important gig for us," he continued. "We could potentially be agented if things go well. That means we would have someone to organize tours and such. It is very tedious and sometimes frustrating having to organize all this ourselves. But we cannot perform to our very best ability without a bassist. Which was why I was wondering if you... if you..."

My brain finally left cloud nine, and everything came clear to me in a rush. "You—you want me to play in your band?"

He nodded. "Sì. I could think of no better person than the lovely, talented woman I just jammed out with." My hands still in his, he rubbed the backs of them with his thumbs.

The question caught me totally off guard. I was thinking of relationships, but he was thinking about music through and through! He really was a man after my own heart. But still, he was putting the pressure on me pretty thick. With the possibility of agents and scouts attending his next gig, that meant the performance needed to be absolutely perfect. How could I possibly be of any help when I'd never even rehearsed with the rest of his band? "When do you guys play? And where?"

"Eight o'clock at Soho 42 jazz lounge, which is in the eastern part of town. "

I shook my head at the absurdity of it all. "This is unreal. I don't even know all of your songs. I've never rehearsed with the rest of your band, so how will I expect to be ready to play for such an important gig?"

He smiled reassuringly. "I believe in you, Trina. Your skills are amazing, from what I have seen and heard. Besides, you have such a great memory, knowing our songs just from attending a couple of our shows."

"But I still need to rehearse—"

"We can rehearse a little before the show tomorrow. All you have to do is play the bass parts the same way you played today."

It sounded easy enough, but I still wasn't too fond of the idea that I might risk ruining everything he and his friends had worked so hard to achieve. "I need some time to think about this."

He sighed. "I understand with it being such short notice. But our group will not sound the same without a bassist, and you have more than proven your skills." When he saw that he hadn't convinced me, he continued, "I will wait in the lobby around four o'clock tomorrow afternoon, in case you change your mind."

He wasn't giving up. He was really leaving the future of his band—and, to some extent, his career— up to me.

CHAPTER 8

I SLEPT WAY TOO WELL AFTER MY "DATE" WITH Samuele. I was up bright and early before the sunrise, thinking about his once-in-a-lifetime offer to play in his band for a very important event. Was it really a stroke of good luck, or was it fate? It seemed too good to be true, and I was already thinking of the worst-case scenario. Maybe I would get stage fright and botch every note. Or I might somehow forget the song and stand there looking like a fool. I shuddered at the thoughts continuously racing through my mind.

But then I reminded myself that it *was* a once-in-a-lifetime opportunity, and I should live life to the fullest, even if things didn't go smoothly. How many people could say that they'd played in a band with a real-life Prince Charming? I smiled.

I was too caught up in my thoughts to bother going out. That guilty feeling of not abiding by my planner that was chock-full of things to do haunted the back of my mind. But it wasn't too often that I would get swept off my feet by a handsome prince who, in less than a week, had managed to turn my world upside down. Of course, I called Claudia during my internal debate with myself, hoping to get a second opinion, even though I had a feeling what she would say.

"What is there to think about?" she exclaimed. "You *better* go play with him! Are you crazy?"

I swallowed. "I want to, but… it's been forever since I played in a band. This isn't like back in college. These are professionals who get paid and have an opportunity to land a deal with an agent or scout. I don't want to be the one who ruins that opportunity."

"What are you talking about? You're an amazing bassist, Trina. I've heard you play. I know you won't mess up."

"Playing alone isn't the same as playing with a group. You have to make sure everyone's on cue, and—"

"Hey, stop thinking about it. Just go and play with him, girl. This is your chance to shine. Who knows when the opportunity will come again, if ever. Besides, are you *really* going to turn down a prince's offer?"

I pursed my lips. I certainly didn't want to, but…

"Just so you know, Stefano and I plan to come to that show, too. And we're going to sit front and center. So you better show up, or I'll be very disappointed."

I gasped. "What!"

"You heard me."

"Great. Way to put the pressure on me, Claudia. Geez." I sighed heavily. "Fine. Fine, I'll do it."

"I knew you would, girl. See you tonight!"

We ended the call, and I stared at the lit-up screen with Claudia's number until the screen finally dimmed off.

Later that afternoon, I paced around my suite, my nerves on edge as if they were being continuously jolted with electric shocks. I'd already told Claudia I was going, but I hadn't told Samuele my decision. But when he saw me in the lobby in five minutes, he would know my answer.

I'd chosen the last dress I'd packed, a white halter cocktail dress, and matching shoes, and put a little makeup on. But even though I was ready to go, I remained planted by the front door. I rested my hand on the handle, sighed, and closed my eyes for a moment. My thoughts shifted to the future possibilities that this one gig might open up for me. What if the scouts and agents liked me and wanted to represent me? Then I could officially be considered a professional musician like my idol, Daisy Weatherspoon. After all, she'd started out as a homeless nobody before a random stranger discovered her while she was playing her acoustic guitar on the street and offered her a music deal. She'd become one of the most famous musicians in America.

I would love to have the same luck, but I figured I'd pretty much used up all my luck on winning the trip and meeting a prince. Every star in the universe would have to be aligned for me to get a music deal just from being a fill-in.

Taking another deep breath, I turned the handle and left my room. I had no more regrets, no more worries. Whatever was bound to happen would happen, good or bad. And I was prepared. The elevator ride down to the lobby seemed like an eternity. I found Samuele at his usual spot by the front desk, chatting with hotel staff. He spotted me, and a look of relief immediately appeared on his face. He swept to my side and took my hands in his.

"Oh, Trina, I am so happy you decided to do this," he said in one breath.

"Yeah, but I'm still nervous…"

"Everything will be fine." He paused and looked me up and down. "You look *bellissima*, as always."

"Thank you." My smile grew after his slight reassurance.

Samuele drove us in his cool white sports car to Soho 42, which was only a ten-minute ride across town. During the trip, he informed me of every song the band intended to play, detailing my parts. It sounded easy enough, but I felt I would be more assured with the rehearsal beforehand.

We pulled up to the venue, a simple brick building on the corner. Like many of the other places I'd seen, the exterior wasn't very flashy, but I could only imagine how the interior looked. A lone metal sign that said Soho 42 sat above the metal door of the hole-in-the-wall establishment. The place looked abandoned, with no one waiting outside, but there *were* over two hours before the club opened for business, so I was sure that would all change soon enough.

We parked in the alley with a few other cars then headed through the side door, which led to a dressing room. Instrument cases, duffel bags, and equipment were strewn about the room. Samuele had only his drumsticks and a tiny bag of various drum supplies, which he set on the floor with the other bags. We left the dressing room and neared the backstage, where I immediately heard a keyboard and saxophone playing. It sounded like Vincenzo and Marco were already rehearsing. Samuele and I came out from backstage, and they stopped playing.

I got a good look of the main part of the club from the stage. From where I stood, it looked like the place could seat over a hundred people—much more than Heaven and Blues. A large bar area sat in the back, and some of the club's staff walked about sweeping the floors, cleaning the bar, and tidying up the numerous round tables and chairs that made up the main seating area of the club. The staff were too engrossed in their work to pay attention to us on stage.

"*Ciao!*" Vincenzo greeted.

I smiled and waved. "Hello." I cast a glance at Marco.

"*Grazie* for doing this, Trina," Marco said.

"Sì! You do not know how important this night is," Vincenzo added.

"I think I have an idea," I said. "So are we going to rehearse or what?"

"Sì." Vincenzo gestured to an electric jazz bass sitting on a stand. It was already on and plugged into the sound system with the other instruments.

I retrieved the instrument then plucked the strings to ensure it was tuned.

"It is all tuned and ready for you," Marco said, as if hearing my thoughts. "I also have the fretless one, if you desire to play that instead." He pointed to an instrument case sitting nearby.

My eyes widened. *Did he really bring Purple Daisy?* After playing with it at the store, I kind of liked it more than my fretted one. *You only live once.* I quickly switched to the fretless, and once I'd gotten all tuned up, we began rehearsing for the show.

By seven thirty, we'd rehearsed the entire two-hour set, nonstop. I'd memorized most of the songs during my jam session with Samuele, and I'd quickly picked up the rest. His bandmates were great to play with, and adapting to their style was easy. These guys had great dynamics, and I was able to complement their sound just the way they wanted. Samuele and Claudia had been right—I was stressed and worried over nothing.

After making one final sound check, we headed backstage to wait until it was time for us to perform. I learned that there was another band scheduled to play after ours. I sensed my bandmates' nervousness—even Samuele seemed anxious—and my heart started pounding as time ticked by. Samuele eventually left and poked his head around the corner. I followed him then mentally kicked myself for doing so because my nerves were completely shot when I noticed that it was a full house. I gulped. *Oh great. Now the pressure is* really *on.*

"See that table there?" Samuele muttered, gesturing with a subtle nod. I followed his direction to a large round table center-right of the stage, where three men and two women dressed in crisp suits and stylish cocktail dresses sat.

"Are those the talent scouts?" I asked.

"Sì. And the woman in yellow is an agent."

I looked at the middle-aged woman wearing the yellow one-shoulder dress and a black sheer scarf draped around her shoulders. She sat back in her chair and chatted with her companions at the table as she sipped from a glass of sparkling gold liquid. She seemed like the friendly sort. I just hoped that our performance would be enough to impress her.

Claudia and Stefano were sitting at a small table for two, front and center of the stage, just as she'd warned. While they talked, Claudia occasionally looked toward the stage. *Probably making sure I don't chicken out.*

"*Mi scusi, si sta eseguendo in cinque minuti.*"

Samuele and I both started at the closeness of the voice and turned to find a man in a black pinstripe suit. He looked like someone important. *The owner, perhaps? Where did he come from?*

Samuele nodded to the man, who mentioned something else to Samuele in Italian. Samuele's eyes went wide. "*Cosa!*"

Smiling, the man patted Samuele on the back and left.

Confused, I looked from the man, who stopped by a table occupied by a couple, to Samuele. "Who was that? What did he say?"

He heaved a deep sigh and looked at me worriedly. "That is the manager. He said at some point in our show for us to allow the audience a chance to give some requests."

I widened my eyes, too. "What!"

"That is exactly what I said."

"We can't do requests. I haven't rehearsed anything but the set list."

"I know, *bella...*"

My heart raced faster. "I don't know if I can do this—not without messing up your one opportunity..."

He looked at me fully and put both hands on my shoulders. He drew his face close to mine. My throat tightened with anxiousness that coursed through my veins. His glasses brought out the beautiful emerald green of his eyes. "Listen to me. You can do this. I believe in you, Trina. My heart has never beat so strongly for someone other than you. I… I think I am falling in love with you."

My mouth fell open. I wanted to pinch myself because it sounded too good to be true. No real Prince Charming would confess his love to an ordinary person like me, would he? The words resonated in my ears over and over again.

But the words came clearer in my head, and I suddenly felt his lips on mine. My eyelids fluttered closed, and I indulged in his delectable royal taste that I'd missed so much.

And yet again, just like that, the kiss was over before it began. I opened my eyes, and he gazed deeply at me.

I stared back at him, still savoring his lingering taste on my lips. *No,* I told myself. *I can't get involved with a bandmate, even if I am just a fill-in. We all know how the last one turned out. Wasn't there a rule or something about never dating bandmates?*

But Samuele wasn't just an average band guy. He was a Prince Charming—*my* Prince Charming. The struggle was real.

"Trina?" he said softly with concern, probably noticing how flustered I was.

I blinked out of my thoughts and focused on him again. "I'm sorry, what were we talking about again?"

His face softened, and he released me. "Nothing, *bella.* Come. We better get ready for the show."

We gathered Vincenzo and Marco from backstage and headed onstage to our stations. Samuele approached Marco and Vincenzo, muttered something to them, and returned to his drums. Based on the pale looks on Marco's and Vincenzo's faces afterward, he'd filled them in on the fact that we were taking requests. But there was no backing out. The stage lights glared down on us like beacons. I could feel all eyes on us, and the low murmurs of the crowd slowly faded out. I locked gazes with Claudia, and she gave me a thumbs-up. For good luck, I supposed. I took a deep breath.

"Psst."

I looked over my shoulder at Samuele, who had his drumsticks up and ready to strike down on his snares and cymbals. He mouthed the title to the first song. I nodded and remembered what we'd rehearsed. He started it off, and the rest of the band fell in time. I kept my eyes averted from the audience while I played, not wanting to worry about their reactions and risk messing up my parts. I silently hoped and prayed that our music would live up to the audience's standards, especially the agent's and scouts'.

Toward the middle of the song, I glanced at Samuele and discovered him looking right back at me. His hands seemed to move autonomously across the drums and cymbals. His attention on me made my cheeks get hot. *Was he watching me all this time?* Feeling his gaze constantly on me and knowing how much he believed in me gave me a small boost of confidence. It was enough for me to play my part a little more creatively than we'd rehearsed, ad-libbing here and there to help bring out the richness of the song. Vincenzo, Marco, and Samuele seemed to enjoy it, because they couldn't stop smiling at me. Suddenly, my fears and worries went away. All the smiles, the good times we were having playing on stage, and the camaraderie reminded me of my old college bandmates. I missed those days. *If only they could see me now.*

We were apparently a hit. Though I couldn't see the audience's facial expressions, their enthusiastic applause at the end of the song spoke volumes. The agent and scouts clapped, too. I wondered what they thought about us so far.

By nine forty-five, we were on the last song of the set. The song started out with a solo sax part. I waited for Vincenzo's cue. It never came. He walked to the standing mic and addressed the audience.

"*Che ne dite di una richiesta da parte del pubblico!*" he said cheerily, though I could hear a slight underlying nervousness in his voice.

I furrowed my brow, then noticed a few audience members raise their hands. One of them was the agent.

I blinked. *Oh no…* It was time for the audience to make requests. I hoped Vincenzo wouldn't choose the agent. She would most likely request a song I'd never heard of, much less know how to play. But I was grateful that he waited until the very end of our set to do it, so we only had time to do one requested song.

"*Ah, la signora in giallo!*" Of course, Vincenzo chose the agent. She fixed her scarf and beamed as if she'd just won the lottery.

My hands started to feel clammy. *At this rate, I won't be able to play properly.* I looked over at Samuele, wondering if he had any bright ideas. But he simply stared ahead at Vincenzo, focused and waiting.

The agent raised her half-filled wine glass. "*Una Favola Tipo di Amore, per favore!*" she said in a bubbly tone. A few audience members clapped and cheered at her suggestion.

Great. Not only did I not know what she'd said, but I also definitely would not be able to play whatever it was. Vincenzo turned and faced us. A look of confusion crossed his pinched face. Marco looked from him, to me, to Samuele, then he shrugged.

Samuele looked back at his bandmates, frowned, and shook his head with a look of defeat.

I left my station and went to Samuele. "What song does she want us to play?"

He pursed his lips. "Something called 'A Fairytale Kind of Love.' We are not sure how it goes."

I blinked. "You're not talking about the same song by Purple Daisy, are you?"

He cocked his head. "Who is that?"

"Only my most favorite American music idol ever!" "A Fairytale Kind of Love" was a drum-and-bass–dominated jazz song with minor piano, trumpet, and sax chords sprinkled throughout. I gave the guys a brief explanation of what they needed to do, then we kicked off the song.

Playing the song all over again reminded me of our date at the music store. I imagined playing the song before Samuele again. The rest of the guys came in on cue. Our rendition sounded great. I inadvertently looked over toward the agent and scouts. All of them were grinning and bobbing their heads, especially the agent, who even tapped her fingers on the table in time to the beat. I shifted my gaze to Samuele, who beamed back at me, looking as proud as ever. My heart swelled with relief that the four of us could play on a whim. It was a sign that we all meshed together as bandmates. I wished I could keep playing with them. But reality suddenly struck my mind. I would be leaving Bellacigna the next day. I would never see these guys again, much less play in a band with them.

We ended the song and took a bow. The audience stood, clapping wildly. My bandmates were beaming. I guessed they knew that the show was a huge success. The agent and scouts looked particularly amazed at the four of us.

Vincenzo turned to the rest of us. "Good job, everyone," he mouthed over the noise, then gave a thumbs-up.

We headed backstage with our instruments—Samuele with his drumsticks—and had a post performance celebration.

"Did you see their faces?" Marco said, still grinning from ear to ear.

"They really liked you guys," I said. "You all will definitely get representation from this."

Samuele cast me a curious look. "They liked you, too, Trina."

I looked back at him, a little sad. "I was just a fill-in. They don't know I'm leaving tomorrow." I began carefully setting the fretless back into the case. I was going to miss that bass. But the memories I'd made with it would be forever etched in my mind.

Vincenzo and Marco gasped. "What? You are leaving? Why?" Vincenzo asked.

"Because my vacation is over," I replied, closing the case and flipping the multiple locks closed. "I live in America—Columbia, South Carolina, to be exact. I work full-time as a barista."

Vincenzo and Marco continued looking at me with a mix of shock and sadness. Samuele never took his eyes off me. I'd already warned him that the day would soon come.

Annoyed by all the staring, I faced the guys. "Look, I really appreciate the wonderful time. This has been the most memorable vacation ever. I've done so many great things and met so many great people. Thank you, guys, for this once-in-a-lifetime opportunity."

Marco sighed then turned to secure his keyboard case. Vincenzo did the same for his tenor sax. The air had suddenly shifted from happy and excited to gloomy. It was almost eleven thirty, and I was ready to get out of there. "Samuele, can you please take me back to the hotel?"

Samuele nodded. "Sì." He said something briefly in Italian to Vincenzo and Marco, who nodded in turn, then he escorted me out the back door. We got in Samuele's car, and he took the wheel. We drove out of the alley and to the main street, where I spotted Claudia and Stefano hanging out in front of the club. "Hey, wait, let me see Claudia first, please," I said to Samuele.

"*Certo*." He parked along the curb not far from the entrance, and I hopped out. Claudia spotted me right away and hurried over. We met halfway in a big hug.

"What a great show!" she said, not releasing me from the hug.

"Thanks," I said through short breaths. "Ugh, you're squeezing the life out of me."

She chuckled and let me go. "Sorry. So you're headed back to the hotel?"

"Yeah, I need to pack and get ready for my flight tomorrow afternoon. Think I can see you before then?"

"Absolutely! In fact, we'll meet for some good old-fashioned gelato."

I grinned. "Sounds like a plan."

A hint of sadness crossed her face. "I can't believe you're really going to be leaving tomorrow."

"Me, neither. But unfortunately, all good vacations must come to an end."

"Can I convince you to move here with me?" She batted her eyes and gave me an innocent look.

"You know I would if I could, but I don't have a means to live out here. You have an excuse—you're married to a duke." I glanced at Stefano, who was standing next to Samuele's car, chatting with Samuele through the rolled-down window.

"What? You mean Samuele didn't propose to you yet?" Claudia asked in a joking tone.

I made a small fake laugh. Deep down, I'd thought something more could have become of us, but perhaps it wasn't the time, but it would be too late once I left. "He's a musician, Claudia. He doesn't have time to propose."

"Okay, you made a point. Still, I can't believe your handsome prince hasn't managed to convince you to stay here."

"Maybe it's for the best." I looked back at Samuele's car. "Hey, I better go. I'll see you tomorrow sometime. Text me when you want to meet."

"Will do." She walked with me back to the car. I got in the passenger's seat and buckled in, while Claudia returned to Stefano and the two of them wrapped their arms around each other and smiled. They were such an adorable couple. A hint of sadness crept through my heart as I watched them.

We said our goodbyes and drove off. The ride back to the hotel was short and silent. Samuele parked at the entrance, shut off the car, and looked at me, his face riddled with sadness and pain. "That was a great concert, *bella. Grazie* for agreeing to play."

I tried to smile, but it was hard, knowing it was perhaps the last time I would see him. "I had fun."

"You are a very talented bassist. I hope you will stick with it."

"I certainly will." *In the comfort of my own home.* I wouldn't be interested in playing with another band after that performance. Playing with Samuele and his friends had been even better than my college group.

A long silence fell between us. He looked at me carefully, then his eyes fell to my lips. *Yes, one last kiss, please...*

"I wish you could stay longer," he finally said. "I am going to miss you." Without giving me a chance to respond, he leaned in and planted a deep, invigorating kiss on my lips. I closed my eyes and enjoyed the moment as I had the others, hoping it would last a little longer than the rest. His taste, his warmth, and his love made my heart swell.

We finally broke the kiss, and I got out of the car. Before closing the door, I looked back at him. The sadness and pain in his face returned. His mouth opened slightly, as if he were about to say something, but he never did. Perhaps he was wrestling the many questions in his mind. But I spared him the decision when I turned and headed for the revolving door.

CHAPTER 9

MY EYES BURNED AS I ZIPPED UP MY GARMENT bag and secured the rest of my luggage. I couldn't believe that my fabulous Bellacignan vacation was officially over. It was time to say goodbye to the fairytale and finally wake up to my normal, everyday life. My flight was scheduled to leave at three o'clock in the afternoon. My anxiety over Wednesday morning made me get up bright and early. But I also couldn't stop thinking of the previous night's successful gig. It was the most memorable point in my life—a memory that I knew I would never make again.

Around nine o'clock, my cell phone rang. *Probably Claudia calling to hash out the details of our final meet-up.* "Hey, girl," I answered cheerily.

"Trina?"

I stiffened at the sound of Samuele's voice on the other end. "Whoa! S-Samuele?"

"*Scusa.* I hope I am not disturbing you."

"No, it's okay."

"Do you have a few minutes to talk?"

The urgency in his voice drew my concern. "Sure. Is everything okay?"

"Sì. I wanted to tell you the good news. Vincenzo said he and Marco talked with the agent and scouts for a while last night. They were all very impressed with our performance."

I smiled. "I knew they would be from the looks on their faces."

"But that is not even the good news. The agent, *Signora* Ines Hearne, wants to sign our band and book a month-long European tour next year."

There was a moment of silence. I blinked several times. "A European *tour*? Are you serious? That's amazing, Samuele! I'm so happy for you!"

"*Grazie.* I am going to talk to her later and see if a portion of the tour's proceeds can go to a charity."

"That would be wonderful. I'm glad you're living your dream, Samuele." The words sounded slightly bittersweet to my ears.

He paused a moment. "Trina… Signora Hearne loved our group—including you."

"Did Vincenzo or Marco tell her that I was a fill-in for Castello, your regular member?"

"Sì, they did, but that did not seem to matter to her. I think she was most impressed by you because you knew the song she requested."

I frowned. "Why should that matter?"

"I do not know how these things work, *bella*. I just know that Signora Hearne is a very reputable agent in the music industry, and the fact that she really likes you is a big statement. That is why I am hoping you might consider staying here and joining the band for good. And doing what you love to do."

My heart jumped to my throat. "What! You know I can't do that. I have a life in America." *A life of making coffee for half-awake, cranky, ungrateful people.*

"But you are such a talented musician. You can make a living doing this and traveling around the world, seeing new places."

The offer sounded tempting. Very tempting. *I could travel around the world with my Prince Charming.* "I would love to, Samuele. But I can't just up and move on a whim."

"Why not?"

"Well, money, for one, and I have a job and bills to pay. And according to Claudia, there's a lot of paperwork involved with moving to another country."

"I can always help you with the moving and paperwork. And I am sure the agent can help you with all the legalities and things."

His insistence was sweet, but he just didn't understand. "I'm sure everything will be fine when Castello comes back."

I heard him sigh. "No, I am afraid it will not. We will still be without a bassist even when Castello comes back."

"Why? Marco plays bass."

"Sì, but he is going to be leaving the band."

I widened my eyes. "*What?*"

"As much as he enjoys playing with us, his true love is with *Dolce Sinfonia Negozio di Musica*. It has been owned and run by his family for several generations. His father passed down the responsibilities to him. Marco will not be able to balance those duties with a music career that involves constant traveling. It was a hard decision for him to make, but I respect his choice. I love him like a brother. We have been at this for a long time."

"I see…"

"He has been very impressed by your skill. All of us have."

I clenched my jaw as the subject reared its ugly head again. My mind and heart were torn yet again over what to do. I wanted to accept his offer, but I was too scared of the outcome. What if I moved all the way over and things didn't work out? I didn't want to be stuck and helpless thousands of miles away from home. I just wasn't ready to gamble my livelihood. "You'll just have to find someone else. I'm sorry."

He sighed again. "Right. I understand. Well, I will miss you very much, Trina." There was a pause. "I meant what I said last night that I have fallen in love with you."

I felt about to cry again. Not because of hearing his sweet confession but because those same words were somehow on the tip of my tongue, too. Part of my mind had warned me that I was in for some serious heartbreak if I got too attached. *Now I'm paying the price.* "I... I..." I formed the L-word with my tongue, but my internal struggles prevented me from fully expressing my heart's desire. "I have to go now. Thank you for making my vacation unforgettable."

I was met with silence on the other end, and I wondered if perhaps he hung up on me. But then I heard a small breath, and I sighed with relief. "Okay.

I hope you have a safe trip back to America." His voice wavered as if he were about to cry himself. Thankfully, we said our goodbyes and ended the call before that happened. I stared at his number on the lit-up phone screen and sighed.

I made the right decision, I kept telling myself. But I felt a great weight of regret pressing down on me.

At 11:30, I checked out of the hotel and went to Cittàcigni for the last time to meet with Claudia for our gelato date. I brought my luggage with me. I called Erudito and asked him to pick me up in an hour. Claudia had taken her lunch break earlier than usual, and there was a nice little *gelateria* within walking distance of the university. Of course, I told her about my phone conversation with Samuele, and of course, as usual, she didn't make things any easier for me.

"How could you refuse that offer, girl? This is your big break! You can do what you've always wanted to do and make an honest living from it. Not to mention see the world."

I inhaled a spoonful of cherry-flavored gelato. "You make it sound so simple. You had a reason to move here. You needed a job, and Stefano was waiting for you. I, on the other hand, already have a job, and Samuele is pursuing his own goals."

She gave me an "are you serious" look. "If I recall, you were the one who submitted my resume on my behalf to the university. I didn't tell you to do that. I didn't even have any intentions of moving here, despite Stefano."

"But you did, and it all worked out," I argued. "Samuele is an established, professional musician. I just play for fun. There's a difference. I just don't see my joining his band working out in the long run."

Claudia crossed her arms. "And why not?"

Because I'll end up falling in love with him and not be able to concentrate on the music. Frowning, I slowly stirred my remaining gelato.

"I know what it really is, Trina," Claudia said, and I gave her a blank look. We knew each other like a book. I didn't know why I'd ever attempted to hide something so important from her. "You're afraid to fall in love with a guy halfway across the world. Well, you know what? You already have, and there's nothing you can do about it but follow your heart. You can't be a barista for the rest of your life, so stop using that as an excuse. You've had that same job since college. It's time for a change."

I managed a small smile. Of course, she was right. Of course, I should follow my heart. But the idea of moving to another country and starting a brand-new life still sounded intimidating.

Claudia cocked her head. "C'mon, Trina. If you move here, then we can finally be together again and see each other everyday. You're the closest to a sister that I have, and I hate that you live so far away and we can't hang out all the time like we used to."

My heart fluttered as I thought about all the good times we had during our college years. "Yeah, I love you, too, Claudia."

We enjoyed the rest of our gelato. It was almost twelve thirty, and Claudia needed to head back to the university. We left the *gelateria*, and I spotted Erudito leaning against the hood of his limousine parked out front, chatting on the phone. He spotted us and quickly ended the call.

"*Buon pomeriggio, signore.*" He tipped his black chauffeur's hat.

Claudia gave him a small wave. "Hi, Erudito. Looking good as always. Tell Adelina 'hi' for me."

Erudito beamed. "*Grazie.* And I will." He turned to me. "Are you ready to leave, Signorina Mauer?"

I chewed my bottom lip and looked from him to Claudia. This was it. Claudia looked back at me with sad eyes. We shared a big hug and said our final goodbyes. I returned to Erudito. "I'm ready."

"Okay." He opened the back door for me, and I climbed into the limo. I spotted a colorfully wrapped present sitting on the opposite seat. There didn't appear to be any name on it, so I left it alone. After packing my luggage in the trunk of the limo, Erudito returned to the driver's seat. "Next stop, the airport."

I stared out the window at Claudia, who stood at the curb, waving, with a sad smile. I waved back at her, but I wasn't sure if she could see me through the heavily tinted window. I didn't take my eyes off her as we drove away. Her image became smaller the farther we drove. Soon, we rounded a corner, and she was out of sight.

"Ah, Signorina." Erudito's voice broke the silence. I looked at him through the rearview mirror. His gaze met mine briefly. "Signora Stacson left a small parting gift for you."

"You mean this one on the seat?" I cast another glance at the mysterious box.

"Sì. And she wishes you all the best and hopes to see you again very soon."

I retrieved the small present. It was wrapped with cupcake-printed paper and tied with a bright-pink bow. I smiled at the thought of what was probably inside. *Planner decorations. What else?* I'd gone completely rogue on my planner during the vacation, but I was sure to return to my old nerdy self once I got home. I carefully unwrapped the gift.

I blinked at what I discovered inside. It wasn't planner decorations. Not a single sticker or inch of washi tape. No, it was something even more amazing—one of her books! I swallowed and studied the title. "*Un Bel Tramonto.*" Underneath the title, it said, "A Beautiful Sunset —English Edition." I furrowed my brow. I'd never heard of the book before.

Erudito looked at me in the rearview mirror. "That book is an English-edition advance reading copy of Signora Stacson's newest book," he said, as if hearing my thoughts. "It is slated to be released this autumn. You have the very first printed edition."

I widened my eyes, and my jaw dropped open. Adelina's next book, first edition! I carefully flipped through the pages, inhaling the addicting, new-book smell of the pages. She'd written a message at the front of the book:

"*Per Trina: Sempre credere in te stesso e seguire il vostro cuore.* (Always believe in yourself and follow your heart.) —M.E."

My cheeks hurt from smiling so much. Adelina had put the final cherry on top of the memorable vacation.

CHAPTER 10

I RETURNED TO COLUMBIA, SOUTH CAROLINA, around four o'clock Thursday afternoon. By five thirty, I was back in my one-bedroom apartment. I didn't bother unpacking. I sent Claudia a quick text, letting her know I was back and headed straight to bed. I intended to return to work bright and early the next morning. Back to Trina's normal life. But somehow, after returning from the much-needed vacation, my old life didn't seem too appealing anymore.

The jetlag wasn't much help when I got up early for work Friday morning. But it wouldn't take long for my body to get back into the swing of things. I dragged my feet down to Lala Latte, thinking about my trip, the wonderful people I'd met, the amazing gifts I'd received, and my last conversation with Claudia.

Arriving at work, I was surprised to see my boss's car parked in the lot. Grace and her husband usually didn't come in until later in the morning or afternoon. I peered in the office's doorway and saw her doing paperwork. I knocked softly on the open door. "*Ciao!*" I greeted in my weak attempt at Italian.

Grace looked up, her aged face creasing with lines as she smiled. "Oh, Trina! Welcome back!" She got up from the desk and gave me a big hug.

Grinning, I hugged her back. Her kind demeanor always reminded me of my late grandmother. I guessed that familiarity was why I'd always enjoyed working for her. When we broke the hug, I pulled out a small wrapped gift—a musical statuette of the *Teatro all Diamante*—from my purse. "Got you a souvenir."

"Thank you." She graciously took the colorful box and set it on her desk. She looked at me again, and I noticed a slight pinch in her brow. She took my hands and rubbed them gently. "Trina, before you clock in for work, I would like to talk to you."

Eyeing our clasped hands, I felt my throat tighten. *Well, this is a first.* I looked at her with slight concern. *Did something happen while I was gone?* "Sure. What's up?" I tried to sound optimistic.

She led me to the empty chair at the desk and gestured for me to sit. Afterward, she closed the office door. She paced around for a moment then stopped in front of me. "There's nothing to worry about. Everything here is just how you left it."

I nodded, slight tension leaving my body.

"You've been working here throughout your entire college life and several months after. This has nothing to do with your work ethic. You are the hardest worker here, and I love you very much like a daughter."

"Thank you." I smiled.

"*But* I think it's about time that you finally take that next step and enter your career. I've had a lot of job inquiries from current college students who are struggling with bills, and I would like to help them. Which is why…"

"You're firing me," I finished in one breath.

She pursed her lips. "No, I'm not firing you. I just want to give you the opportunity to pursue the career that you spent so much time and effort getting a degree for. I helped you when you were a struggling college student. Now it's time for me to help another.

I still have and always will love you like my own daughter, Trina. I just want the very best for you."

Somehow, I'd sensed something like this would eventually happen, which was why I'd been building up a nest egg to sustain me for six months. *So what was I so afraid of?*

Failing. What if my music career didn't work out? What if all those years of studying were a waste? What would I have to fall back on? I swallowed, dwelling on the worst-case scenario.

That night, I called Claudia. "I guess I could try and get a job at the music department at USC. It's just... after your stroke of bad luck with the job-hunting situation, I'm not sure that I'll—"

"Girl, this is perfect! Come out here with me!"

I blinked. "What!"

"There's nothing holding you back now. It's the perfect opportunity to start that new life and career."

I sighed softly. Deep down, I'd thought she would say something like that. The thought of returning to Bellacigna and seeing Samuele again wasn't too far from my mind, either. "And what about a job?"

"Didn't you say Samuele and his band—you included—got a huge music deal?"

"Yeah, but I don't want to rely solely on that. Anything can happen from now until the tour date."

"Well, you can work at the university with me. Stefano's new music program is amazing. There's already a job waiting for you here—as well as your very own office."

I thought about her offer. Maybe the idea of living in a magical place like Bellacigna wasn't so farfetched after all. Maybe I was just getting all worked up over nothing. Maybe making another new life with my best friend—and possibly my Prince Charming—really *was* possible.

I thought about Adelina's note to me in her first-edition book. *"Always believe in yourself and follow your heart."* I rubbed my chin. Life was short. I needed to jump in while the opportunity was there. My fear had kept me at Lala Latte for almost six years. *Wow. Have I really been working here for that long?*

"So? You coming or what?" Claudia asked again, and I realized I hadn't responded to her last comment.

"I need to think this over," I finally said.

"Yeah, whatever. I'll get your new office all set up." I could hear the smile in her voice.

Geez, she knows me way too well...

Erudito stopped in front of Adelina's villa and opened the door for me. I grabbed my purse and got out quickly. A bright smile spread across my face when I saw one of the maids waiting at the front door of the villa. It didn't seem like four months had passed since I was last there. But with Claudia and Samuele's help, I'd finalized all the legal paperwork fairly quickly and made the big move to Bellacigna. Adelina had insisted that I stay with her in her sixteen-bedroom villa, and I couldn't resist. Being in the same house as my favorite author in the world and having unlimited access to the most awesome in-home library I'd ever seen was more than amazing.

Taking Claudia's advice, I decided to work as a music teacher at the University of Cittàcigni. I also contacted Samuele, who sounded ecstatic about the news. He sent along some of the songs that the band had been rehearsing for next year's tour, and I got a head start in practicing. There was no greater opportunity than to start living my dream, and I was going to live it to the fullest.

Erudito followed me inside the villa, toting my two giant suitcases. He must've been very strong beneath that lean frame because he carried my bags so effortlessly. The maid led the way through the house, up a flight of stairs, and finally stopped in front of a dark cherrywood door. She smiled a grandmotherly smile and stepped aside.

"Here is your apartment, Signora Mauer." She gestured with her hand.

I stared at the door for a moment then slowly placed my hand on the brass knob. The maid stood with her hands behind her back. Erudito waited with my bags. I opened the door and was immediately engulfed by bright sunlight cast from the large windows covered by sheer curtains. Entering the large, one-bedroom apartment suite, I sucked in a breath, admiring the bright blues and greens of its beach-themed turquoise walls and curtains. Past a small sitting area and kitchenette was a door with a fragrant decorative moonflower wreath hanging from it. I opened the door and stepped into the breathtaking master bedroom. I adored the continuing beach-themed colors, which found their way onto the linens of the king-size bed, upon which a long wrapped box sat.

A sliding glass door revealed a walk-in closet. It was dark, but the sliver of light from the slightly open door of the adjoining master bath was enough for me to discern that the closet was huge. I quickly returned to the main room.

"This is beautiful," I managed to say.

"Signora Stacson will be very happy to know that this room meets your standards," the maid said.

I whipped around. "Are you kidding? This is overkill. I don't think I ever want to leave this room."

Erudito set my bags down. "The rest of your items will be arriving here over the next few weeks."

I nodded. I'd sold a lot of my things in preparation for the big move and was left with a few personal odds and ends.

Erudito left with the maid, and I was finally alone. I peered out the window, which overlooked part of the courtyard and the landscape beyond the villa. Distant mountains were partially veiled by haze. The cloudless blue sky deemed it a perfect day to be outside. Leaving the window, I returned to the bedroom to investigate the gift. It was probably something from Adelina to welcome me into her home, but when I checked for a card, there was none. Curious, I pulled the red bow loose and unwrapped the gift. I gasped. The smell of jasmine and roses wafted from the box as I uncovered the bundle of flowers. I closed my eyes and inhaled their sweet scent. My thoughts immediately drifted to Prince Charming, the most likely sender. I uncovered the small card tucked in with the flowers. Written in flowing script was a note:

"Come to the courtyard when you have looked in the closet. —Love, Samuele"

I chewed my bottom lip. I stared at that four-letter word in his closing for several moments, letting it sink into my brain. *Love.* Did he really love me? We hadn't discussed our deepest feelings for each other since I'd left Bellacigna the first time, but I hadn't stopped thinking about it.

I hopped up from the bed and bounded to the closet. When I walked inside, the overhead track lights flipped on automatically. My suspicions about the size of the closet were confirmed. Leaning up against the wall at the back of the bare closet was another long, wrapped box. It was much larger than the flower box but wrapped just as elegantly. I carefully picked up the box, which felt a little heavy, then set it on the floor. I held my breath as I carefully unwrapped it. Then my breath hitched when I uncovered what was inside. *The Purple Daisy fretless! Did Samuele really get this for me?* I picked up a card sitting on top and tried to read it, but the words were wavering beyond the happy tears that stung my eyes. I wiped my eyes with the back of my arm and focused on the note.

"Vivere per la musica. — Love, Samuele"

I ran my fingers over his signature and smiled. I had no choice but to let the happy tears fall.

With Purple Daisy in tow, I rushed out of my room, down the stairs, and to the courtyard, passing a few more startled staff along the way. There, I found Samuele and Adelina sitting together at the table. Samuele was beating on a portable digital drum kit while Adelina watched, sipping a glass of wine. Samuele looked up and suddenly stopped playing. Grinning from ear to ear, he set his drumsticks down and hurried over to me.

Adelina scooted around in her chair and grinned at me as well.

Samuele stared at me for several moments. "Trina…"

I smiled back. "Hi, Samuele. Thank you so much for the gifts. I… I love you, too."

His eyes brightened, and he sealed my declaration with a deep kiss to my lips. "Best news I have heard all day."

He led me to the table with Adelina, who stood from her chair.

"Trina, I am so happy you are finally here again," she said, then gestured to her now-empty seat.

"Thank you, Adelina. I'm so honored to be here," I said.

Samuele furrowed his brow. "Are you not going to stay and listen to our jam session, sister?"

"Maybe later. I have a writing deadline to work on. Besides, I think you two have a lot to catch up on." She gave me a wink.

I chuckled, and she left us alone. I turned back to Samuele. "We *do* have a lot to catch up on—and a lot of rehearsing to do for next year's tour."

"Sì. But first—" He picked up his drumsticks. "I just want to jam with you again like we did on our date at the music store."

I raised my eyebrows. "So is this another date?"

"No, *bella*. This is love."

About the Author

MARIE LONG is a novelist who enjoys the snowy weather, the mountains, and a cup of hot white chocolate. She's an avid supporter of literacy movements like We Need Diverse Books (WNDB) and National Novel Writing Month (NaNoWriMo). To learn more about her, visit her website: www.marielongauthor.com.

www.ingramcontent.com/pod-product-compliance
Lightning Source LLC
Chambersburg PA
CBHW021200110726
47900CB00002B/662